"I suppose you expect a reward now."

From the wallet he extracted three small white cards and pushed them at Selene.

They looked like business cards. Instead of a printed name, a filigreed gold line wrapped itself in a design in the middle of each white rectangle.

"What are they?" Selene asked.

"Wishes," said the elf prince. "You've got three. Just make a wish and burn a card. It doesn't"—he looked her over with contempt—"require a college education."

"Thanks, but no, thanks," said Selene, and handed the cards back.

"An utterly delightful collection of short stories. . . . Each is a perfectly crafted, captivating little gem. Nothing is overdone and not a word is out of place in this auspicious debut."   —*Kirkus Reviews,* pointer review

"The real magic here is Turner's ability to convince readers that the realms of fairy tales can intersect with everyday life."   —*Booklist,* starred review

OTHER PUFFIN BOOKS YOU MAY ENJOY

MEGAN WHALEN TURNER

INSTEAD
OF THREE
WISHES

PUFFIN BOOKS

PUFFIN BOOKS
Published by the Penguin Group
Penguin Putnam Inc., 375 Hudson Street, New York, New York 10014, U.S.A.
Penguin Books Ltd, 27 Wrights Lane, London W8 5TZ, England
Penguin Books Australia Ltd, Ringwood, Victoria, Australia
Penguin Books Canada Ltd, 10 Alcorn Avenue, Toronto, Ontario, Canada M4V 3B2
Penguin Books (N.Z.) Ltd, 182-190 Wairau Road, Auckland 10, New Zealand

Penguin Books Ltd, Registered Offices: Harmondsworth, Middlesex, England

First published in the United States of America by Greenwillow Books, 1995
Reprinted by arrangement with Greenwillow Books,
a division of William Morrow and Company, Inc.
Published in Puffin Books, 1998

1 3 5 7 9 10 8 6 4 2

LIBRARY OF CONGRESS CATALOGING-IN-PUBLICATION DATA
Turner, Megan Whalen.
Instead of three wishes / Megan Whalen Turner.
p. cm.
Summary: A collection of seven stories featuring leprechauns, ghosts, time
travel, and other extraordinary creatures and experiences.
ISBN 0-14-038672-6 (pbk.)
1. Children's stories, American. [1. Supernatural—Fiction. 2. Short stories.]
I. Title.
PZ7.T85565In 1998 [Fic]—dc21 97-50537 CIP AC

Printed in the United States of America

These stories
were written
for Mark Turner

CONTENTS

INSTEAD OF THREE WISHES

A
PLAGUE OF
LEPRECHAUN

Tuesday morning, the *North Twicking Times* of North Twicking, New Hampshire, ran a story on a leprechaun recently sighted by James Fairsidle on his way down to his south field. North Twicking was a town of Irish descent and Fairsidle was a man who'd always longed to see a leprechaun, certain that he could bully the little beggar into releasing his treasure. Now he had seen one, and he had the broken wrist to prove it, having fallen over a stone in his hurry to catch hold of the little green man. As a result, he'd be hiring Patrick Whelan to do his spring plowing for him. He came into Mrs. Malleaster's tavern very grumpy about the whole business and claimed that the leprechaun had magicked the stone under his feet. As this contravened the well-ordered rules of leprechauns, he found very little sympathy among the other midday tavern-goers.

"You'd have done better to keep your mouth shut about the whole business instead of letting the entire world in on what a fool you were," said Mag Malleaster. "I don't know why you did such a silly thing."

"Because Rob down at the paper gives a pretty good fee to anyone who brings in a story, that's why," said Fairsidle. "That money is the only good thing to come out of this business."

"Wouldn't surprise me if it was," muttered Mag, wiping down the bar. "This time tomorrow we'll be overrun."

"I thought you'd like the business, Mag."

"I would if they would come one after another like decent tourists. I've only got six rooms in the inn, haven't I? Mark my words, they'll all be here together, and just as we've ordered in enough beer to keep 'em, they'll all be gone and leave nothing behind but the undrunk Guinness I have to pay for."

North Twicking did its best to prepare, but by the next afternoon there were more leprechaun hunters than you could shake a stick at. They came from near and from far. A cowboy came all the way from Kingsville, Texas. There were old ones and young ones and single ones and ones that brought along their entire families. Mag's inn was filled. The only empty room she had was one that had been reserved several weeks earlier, and she'd been offered a great deal of money by a number of people if she would just cancel that reservation and let them have the room. Each time she'd said no, but it made her hot under the collar to turn down money, and as the day passed, she got more and more snappish. The regulars in the tavern looked carefully into their beers and only spoke when ordering a new round.

"But, madam," one of the visitors pointed out, "leprechauns are good luck."

"No," said Mag, "leprechauns are *lucky*. You don't get good luck without bad, and I'll tell you which kind those little men like to hand out."

Right she was. By the end of the week, all the milk in the county was running sour. The cows closest to North Twicking were the worst. Saturday afternoon the water main in town burst, and folks had to carry their water from the town well. Sunday the Holbins' barn caught fire, and they were lucky to get the animals safely out before it burned to the ground. These were just the larger disasters. Marjorie Sites turned her ankle, Caleb Bates's car got flats in all its tires one right after the other, and Jamie Walsh woke up Monday morning to find that his prize black Angus were scattered all over the Twicking Hills. Mixed in with these events were the six or seven search parties that had to be organized to hunt down missing tourists and their children, all of whom claimed to have been led off by the leprechaun.

Monday afternoon, a young man with a knapsack and a black briefcase walked into the tavern and asked if Mrs. Malleaster was the proprietress of the hotel.

Mag finished pouring the pint she was working on and stared at the bar a moment before she answered. She was, in general, fair-minded, congenial, and kind. Her customers liked her and she made a reasonable living with her tavern.

Still, North Twicking got very few out-of-town visitors, it being much less accessible than South Twicking, located on the highway fifteen miles down the valley. It fairly made her blood boil to have so many potential customers and to have to turn them away. She reached for a slip of paper and slid it across the bar to the young man.

"We're all full up here. That's a list of families who will rent space to visitors, but I'll warn you that the town water main is burst and you won't be able to get a bath at any of 'em. You can use my phone to call around and see who's got room." She turned back to the tap and began filling the next pint.

The young man looked a little stunned, as well he might. He lowered his briefcase to the floor and sidled closer to the bar. "Uh, I don't mean to be rude, but my name is Roger Otterly, and I think I have a room here. I did make a reservation and, uh, I did pay in advance."

"Oh, good heavens!" Mag put the mug down on the bar half full. "What must you think of us? Yes, of course I have your room." She called over her one waitress and said, "Jen, keep an eye on the bar. I'm going to take this young man up to his room. It's right this way, sir."

As she preceded him up the narrow stairs to the second floor, she explained that it was the only room left in the hotel since the leprechaun sighting had brought so many people to town, and she'd had such difficulties reserving it that she'd forgotten that there was a person she was reserving it for. "That little man has brought us more difficulties than blessings, and that's the truth," she said. But Roger Otterly didn't seem much interested in the leprechaun. After pointing out the bath at the end of the hall and reassuring him that the inn pumped water from its own well and water supply was not a problem, Mag headed back to the tavern.

Just as she reached the stairs, however, Roger Otterly poked his head out of his room and asked, "I'm sorry, did you say that there were a lot of people visiting because of this, um, leprechaun person?"

"Yes. You might say they were thicker than currants in pudding. Is that a problem?" she asked when she saw the downcast expression on the young man's face.

Roger stepped around the edge of the doorway and stood with his hands in his pockets as he explained. "I'm an artist, you see. Anyway, I've just gotten out of art school, and I'm sure I'm at the beginning of a long and famous career." He smiled at Mag, and she smiled back. "I've got no money, but I do have a commission to paint six pictures of some charming countryside for a dentist's office. They have to be finished by Friday, and North Twicking was supposed to be the charming countryside."

"And you think it won't be so charming with hordes of picnickers hiking to and fro?"

"I'm afraid that's what the dentist will think. But we'll just have to hope for the best."

The next morning, Roger took his briefcase with his paints and canvases and an easel fitted cleverly inside and hiked up a hill. He settled down to work and found everything even worse than he expected. It wasn't just that there were cars zooming up and down every road in view or that the treasure hunters had left scatterings of trash at every picnic site. These things could be carefully left out of a painting. No, Roger's biggest problem was the treasure hunters themselves, who insisted on stopping to look over his shoulder and distract him from his work with comments like "Gosh that's good, are you an artist?" or worse, "I'm a bit of an artist myself, and I think you've got the wrong color on that barn there." He tried moving to more and more isolated places, but there was nowhere isolated enough with a leprechaun hunt going on. Finally he packed up his paints and went back to the Jaunty Fox for his lunch. He spent the rest of the afternoon in the tavern.

The regulars made room for him happily enough, but after an hour or two they sent Mag over with a beer and a question. She leaned over the table and asked quietly, "Rog, they want to know why you're staring at them." When there was no response to her question, she nudged him sharply with an elbow. "Have you never seen men drink beer before?"

Roger flushed cadmium red to his hairline and stammered, "I don't have a sketchbook with me. I'm always forgetting it. So I have to memorize what people look like in order to draw them later."

Meg looked down at a number of rough sketches on a cocktail napkin. "Can you do that? Keep a picture in your head and draw it later?"

"Well, yes, like I said, I'm always forgetting my sketchpad, so I've had lots of practice. That man with the enormous mole, for instance, I could probably wait a year and still draw it."

"Well, better leave James and his mole off your sketchpad. It might end a budding career. I will tell the other patrons that you're not trying to put the hex on any of them. I don't suppose they mind being models for a great artiste." She winked and went away.

She was right. They were all quite flattered. They invited Roger over and asked him about the artist's life, and after that nobody minded if he got a little unfocused in the middle of a conversation. This was quite a good thing because Roger spent all of Wednesday in the tavern as well. He talked to the customers and sketched rough reminders on Mag's napkins until she supplied him with a telephone pad to work on. While he talked, Jamie Walsh was out looking for his cows again and the Boswells' pigs were running loose as well, mostly through the Sites' cabbage. Two more search parties had to be organized, and everyone with an affliction brought it to the Jaunty Fox to be aired.

There was no sign that the leprechaun frenzy was abating, so it came as something of a shock to Roger the next morning when he came downstairs and found the inn empty of all but Mag and her regulars.

"It's that leprechaun," Mag explained when she met him in the breakfast room. "There's an article in the *Peskaworthy Times* that says it's been sighted there. They say two little girls on the way to school stopped and talked with it but didn't think to ask about any treasure."

"And where is Peskaworthy?"

"Oh, it's a good fifty miles around the Twicking Hills and down the next valley," said Mag, and she smiled as she put out a plate of scones and jam for him.

It was a beautiful day. The sun had burned off the morning softness, and Roger was able to see for several miles once he reached the upper slopes of a suitable hill. He laid out his paints and set up his easel and worked all morning. In the early afternoon his stomach suggested that maybe it was time for a little lunch, and rather than pack up and carry all his supplies down the hill, he decided to leave them where they were. Now that the leprechaun seekers were gone, the fields were empty and the supplies should be safe enough. He closed the lid of the briefcase carefully and headed down to the Jaunty Fox.

It was three o'clock before Roger hiked back up the hill. He'd left the easel and briefcase just above a rock out-cropping, and as he approached the rock, he saw something he hadn't noticed earlier. There was a very pretty drawing on the rock face of a black cow jumping over a small china white moon. It looked so much like one of the old cave paintings sometimes found in these parts that it only dawned slowly on Roger that the painting hadn't been there in the morning, that it was in fact painted with *his* ivory black and *his* china white paints. He hurried past the rocks, and just as he feared, his easel and his paints were in disastrous disarray. The canvases were scattered across the hillside. The one nearest him was lying faceup, and he could see that it was ruined. Someone had splashed paint across it and added a cartoon of a spaceship landing on top of one of the picturesque hills.

More angry than he could remember being in his life, Roger collected up the canvases and as many of the squashed paint tubes as he could find. He swept everything into the briefcase, slammed it shut. He brushed angry tears out of his eyes. Not only was his morning's work wasted, the supplies were gone. Without money to replace them, he couldn't complete his commission. He whirled around, ready to storm back down to the Jaunty Fox and ask Mag who ever would have done such a thing, because he, Roger Otterly, was going to extract monetary reimbursement if he had to commit murder to do it.

Roger stopped his stampede with one foot raised in the air. Then he very slowly lowered that foot to the ground. His anger receded in the face of an artistic challenge. Standing on the rock outcropping below him, looking very pleased with himself, was the most extraordinary little man. His skin was a sort of Naples green, Roger thought, with maybe a touch of burnt sienna in the cheeks. The clothes were definitely cadmium green, but maybe it should be yellow ochre in the cheeks? And was that a snipe feather or a grouse feather in the hatband? Roger stared. The little man said something, but Roger couldn't be bothered to answer. He thought it was probably a snipe feather. He would describe it to the regulars at the Jaunty Fox; they'd be able to tell him what it was. The little man was shouting, but Roger was carefully noting the contrasting color of his boots and his belt. The little man gestured to something hidden behind the rocks, but Roger's eyes were glued to the leprechaun. Finally, with a look of grim disgust the little man pulled a bag from the air behind him and threw it at Roger's feet. He then disappeared, but Roger was happy. He'd had plenty of time to get all the details right. He looked down with a pleased smile on his face and saw the bag on the grass in front of him. He picked it up and looked inside. All the way back to the inn he daydreamed about the paints he was going to buy.

Roger had paid in advance for his room at the Jaunty Fox, so he slipped away in the morning before anyone was awake. Mag found a small change purse left in his room with a note for her pinned to its side. She tucked it into her apron pocket and only remembered it when a customer needed change for a dollar. She pulled out the purse and twisted open the note. "To cover the cost of a long-distance phone call," she read aloud. She snapped open the purse cover and shook out not quarters and nickels and dimes but a single shining gold piece larger than a silver dollar and twice as heavy.

One of the regulars hiked himself onto the bar to look. "That's a little steep for a phone call, isn't it, Mag?" he asked.

"It is," she said. "Especially when it was me that made the only long-distance call this weekend."

"And was that call by any chance to the newspaper over in Peskaworthy, Mag, dear?"

"Never you mind where the call went. The Boswells have their pigs, Jamie Walsh has his cows home, and you can just be glad we're not going to see that blasted leprechaun again." She slipped the coin back into her apron and patted the pocket.

She was right as usual. Leprechauns never stay where they've had to forfeit their treasure. That particular leprechaun has never been seen again except in a series of paintings exhibited later that year by an up-and-coming young artist named Roger Otterly.

LEROY

ROACHBANE

It was still dark outside when the buzzer next to Leroy's bed went off. Without a sound, he slipped out from underneath the covers and hunted for his bathrobe somewhere at the end of the bed. The cold air crinkled his skin with goose bumps before he found it. His shoes, near the bedroom door, were easier to find. They lay in the path of the hallway night-light. Once he had them on, he walked as quietly as he could down the hall to the kitchen. He could hear the building's hot water, heated by the furnace, banging its way up the radiator pipes to his apartment. Soon the pantry off the kitchen would be the warmest room in the building. It would stay warm all day. That's why the roaches liked living there so much. Warmth all winter with water just a quick scrabble away in the unheated kitchen. Food wasn't plentiful, but there was enough nearby to keep a colony going. Life there would be paradise if not for the early-morning arrival of the great and evil destroyer of roaches.

"Waaaaah!" Leroy turned on the light in the pantry and leapt in between the shelves. Stamping his feet and yelling, he thumped and splatted every roach he could see. With a paintbrush (reserved for this purpose) he swept two or three stragglers off the shelves and stamped on those, too. When he was done, and the ground was littered with squashed corpses, he pulled the broom and dustpan from behind the refrigerator and swept up the mess.

"Are you about done in there?" his mama asked from around the corners. She wouldn't come in until all the roaches were gone.

"Just about. Wait one more minute," said Leroy, and dumped the last of the remains into the garbage can.

"How many did you get today?" his mama asked.

"Seventeen," said Leroy proudly.

"Ick. That's an awful lot. Is it a record?"

"No, there used to be lots more when the college students lived next door. There aren't so many now that Mrs. Hansen is there. You can come in now."

Leroy's mama came around the corner. She didn't wear curlers at night, and her hair wasn't in braids, so it floated on top of her head like a lumpy black cloud. She stood yawning in her bathrobe and bare feet. Even in the coldest weather she didn't like to wear slippers, so Leroy got up every morning to remove any roaches she might step on. Leroy's mother said that she could stand a lot of things, but roaches in the morning were more than she could bear.

"You go get dressed and get ready for school, now. I'll get breakfast started. Your clean pants are in the laundry basket in my room. Don't wake your dad." Leroy knew that nothing short of an earthquake would wake his father after an all-night shift. Otherwise he would have been more quiet killing the roaches.

"And hurry, please," Leroy's mother went on. "I'd like you to leave early for school so that you can buy some more boric acid on the way." Boric acid was the white powder that she sprinkled around the base of all the cabinets and underneath the fridge. It didn't hurt people but was deadly to roaches and cheaper than Roach Motels or any of the insecticide sprays.

Leroy liked going to the hardware store, but thinking of school brought a tight, cold feeling to his stomach. His mother must have known what an unhappy stomach looked like from the outside because she asked, "What's the matter, Leroy? Are the older boys bothering you again?"

"No," said Leroy. "I got something from school I have to show you." He walked up the hall to his room and came back with a piece of paper he had pulled from his schoolbag. It was a note from his teacher. At the bottom of the page there was a space for his mother to sign.

Leroy and his mother sat at the kitchen table while she read the paper. He was still dressed in his bathrobe and pajamas and his school shoes with no socks. His ankles were cold.

"Leroy," his mother finally said, "this says that you were supposed to write a report about the life of your African ancestors and you wrote about Sweden and said that's where your white missionary ancestor came from."

"If Curtis can say his ancestor was Shaka, king of the Zulus, how come I can't have a white missionary?"

"Because, Leroy, you were supposed to write about your African ancestors, people that you can be proud of, young man. Even if they were pig farmers and not kings of the Zulus."

"If I'm gonna write about ancestors I'm proud of, how come I don't write about Grampa, who went to Oberlin College, or about my mother, who is a nurse, or about my dad? Aren't I supposed to be proud of them?"

"That's flattering, Leroy, but you were assigned to write about your African ancestors. Your dad and I aren't that old yet."

"But all the books in the public library are about white people from Sweden. Every year we're supposed to write about African ancestors and every year there's only the one book about Africa and everybody writes the same report and it's really stupid. Why don't they have any books about Africans if that's what we're supposed to write about?"

Leroy's mother put the paper on the table. "Well, Leroy, it's because this used to be a community of people who came from Sweden. Back then the library had money to buy books, and they bought the books that the people who lived here wanted to read. Now the library doesn't have any more money to buy books, even though the neighborhood has changed. That's why we have a lot of people whose ancestors are African reading about life in Sweden instead." She sighed.

"But," she went on, "there are books about Africa in

the main library downtown, and that's where we'll go this Saturday. Your teacher says that your report was very inventive and well researched, even if it was on the wrong subject, so she's going to let you write another one. I'll write her a note that says we'll go get some books on the right subject."

"Okay," said Leroy as he watched his mother sign the paper. "But I'm gonna write about pig farmers, not about Shaka."

Riding his bike home from school that day, clutching a bag full of boric acid bottles, Leroy was cheerful. There had been a sale at the hardware store, and he had gotten twice as many bottles of boric acid as well as a box of Roach Motels thrown in free. Leroy's head was still full of facts about Sweden and the north; they seemed appropriate as he bicycled through the snow, but he looked forward to a trip to the main library downtown. In addition to the books on Africa, he hoped to get *The House of Dies Drear* by Virginia Hamilton. The only copy in the school library had disappeared before he had a chance to read it.

Ignoring the cold winter wind as it blew through his jacket, Leroy absentmindedly navigated around snowpiles and ice patches until he reached the alley behind his building. Disaster struck as he turned into his own backyard. He hit an ice patch he hadn't seen and skidded across it. He might have recovered if one hand hadn't been occupied with the paper bag. Without proper steering, the bicycle careened around the corner of the row of garages and struck a pile of bricks that had been left to one side of the sidewalk by the superintendent six months earlier. The bicycle stopped. Leroy didn't. Still clutching the brown bag in his hands, he flew over the handlebars. The last thing he saw was the cloud-filled sky above him before he landed on his head in the snowbank on the other side of the brick pile.

It was the cold that woke Leroy. Snow had slipped inside his collar and was melting there against his neck. Squinting his eyes against the bright sunlight, Leroy sat up and pulled himself out of the snowbank. Looking around him, he saw that the pile of bricks was gone. His apartment building was gone, and so was everything familiar. Leroy was in a forest of tall, thin trees that cast long and even thinner shadows across the unmarked snow.

It took Leroy several moments to realize that he was not alone. Moving through the trees was a group of people covered in heavy furs. Most of the people looked to be not much taller than Leroy. The heavy furs covered them from top to toe. They wore fur caps, and when they lifted their feet from the snow, he saw that they each wore fur boots that reached up to their knees.

Wow, Leroy thought, shivering in his winter jacket, these people know how to keep warm.

As the group approached, Leroy saw that they all were men and seemed to be some sort of hunting party. Many of them carried spears, and an animal that Leroy thought might be a reindeer hung from a pole carried by two men.

I'm dead, thought Leroy. I've died and gone to Sweden.

The leader of the group greeted Leroy and introduced himself. Leroy was a little surprised to understand the man but responded politely.

The man asked, "Are you an evil spirit?" He stared at Leroy and was obviously intrigued with the color of the boy's skin. He and his men all had creamy white skin, with a red mark burned by the cold on each cheek.

"No," answered Leroy.

"An incarnation of a god?"

"No," answered Leroy.

"Then you are a hero?" This was almost a statement, not a question at all.

Leroy thought about this. He knew that the only people who traveled in the legends of Sweden were heroes, spirits, or gods. He thought being a hero might provide an excuse for hanging out in a snowbank miles from nowhere.

"Yeah, that's me," he said, "I'm a hero."

"Ah," said the leader of the hunting party. "Of what are you bane?"

Leroy was stumped for a moment. He realized that to be a hero, one had to have killed some wild animal or a monster. He thought.

"Roaches," he said. "I am Leroy Roachbane." And he stood up and curled his arms like a wrestler as he said it.

"Ahhh," the men in the hunting party murmured, and nodded their heads, "roaches, roaches."

"What's a roaches?" asked the leader. He was not obviously impressed with Leroy's size. Standing up, Leroy was still waist-deep in snow.

"Well," said Leroy, thinking fast, "they're about this tall." He held up his hand to his chest. "And about twice as long. They have six legs and really hard skin called, um"—he searched for the word he'd learned the previous week in science class—"called an exoskeleton."

The hunters were looking suitably impressed. "And they have pincers," Leroy added, "giant pincers on the front."

He held out his arms in front of him and waved them in an imitation.

This was enough for the men. Several in the back shifted uneasily and murmured, "Pincers, pincers." They looked around them as if one of these monsters might actually appear from behind one of the skinny trees. One stepped forward to whisper in the leader's ear.

"Would you like to come to dinner?" the leader asked Leroy.

Leroy accepted the invitation, and after collecting his paper bag, he walked back to the lodge with the hunting party. On the way, he learned that he was in the land of King Wiglaff and that the leader of the hunting party's name was Per. Per was the king's second-in-command.

As they walked, Leroy elaborated on his description. "Roaches are very dangerous," he said. "They operate in packs and have been known to carry off several small children at a time."

"Really?" Per asked, horrified.

Leroy nodded.

He was in the process of describing his single-handed victory over seventeen of these monsters when they arrived at Wiglaff's lodge.

The lodge was a long, low building about twenty feet wide by about forty feet long, built out of roughly arranged logs. Inside, a fire burned in a pit in the center of the main room. Per's hunting party, after depositing their catch outside in the snow, gathered around the fire and shed most of their heavy furs. Per introduced Leroy to the king, explaining to Wiglaff that Leroy came from a distant land called ChicagoIllinoy, inhabited by giant monsters called roaches. After describing a roach, Per leaned forward to whisper something into his king's ear. Wiglaff nodded and said to Leroy, "Welcome, would you like some dinner?"

Dinner was a giant meal, with all of Wiglaff's people crowded into the lodge. Leroy helped himself to a little roast reindeer as well as rabbit and a bird he didn't recognize. In between mouthfuls, he retold his story of combat with seventeen roaches. He explained that it took him a while to work up to that many. He'd started with only two or three roaches at a time, he said.

After dinner, the crowd called out for a man named Schoop. Schoop came forward with his harp and sang a number of songs about local heroes. The last song he sang was about Wiglaff himself and his prestigious lodge. In the song, the lodge was large enough to hold three hundred men, there were trophies on the paneled walls, and the fire pit could roast an entire reindeer easily. Leroy looked around. The room he was in was cramped, and it only had maybe a hundred people in it. He thought the song might be exaggerating about the size, but then he saw that there were no trophies at all on the walls.

Wiglaff spoke when the song was over. "My nephew Per thinks that a hero of your size might be helpful against a scourge of small proportions."

Leroy wasn't sure if he was being insulted, so he said nothing.

Wiglaff gestured to his surroundings and said, "You do not find our lodge to be similar to that one in the song?"

Leroy hemmed and hawed and finally admitted that it seemed a little different.

"It is different," said Wiglaff. "It is a different lodge." He explained. "We had a lodge across the river from here. It was the beautiful lodge described in the song. It took us many years to build, but unfortunately we had to abandon it in the last few days. We haven't been in this lodge long enough to get the trophies up on the wall, so it's a little rustic yet."

"Why did you move?" Leroy asked.

"It was infested," Per said. "Something like your roaches, only very very small. There were thousands of them, though. They climbed all over everything. They were on the food and on the babies. I would wake up in the night and find them crawling across me." Per shuddered. "It was awful."

"We thought," began Wiglaff hesitantly, "that seeing as how you had so much experience with these giant roaches, maybe you could do something about all these little ones?"

"What do you think?" asked Per.

"Sure," said Leroy, "I can handle it."

So he asked for a package of food that would last him a week and some furs to sleep on. Wiglaff and Per gave him directions to the old lodge, and he started off the next morning with his bag of Roach Motels and boric acid under his arm. He crossed a shallow river, stepping carefully on the stones set out just for that purpose. He climbed a snow-covered hill and found the lodge just on the other side.

Wiglaff's old lodge was significantly larger than his new one and quite a bit more impressive. The huge double doors at one end were covered with the carvings of forest animals and hunting parties. Leroy was afraid that they might be too heavy for him to move, but he pushed one, and it swung open easily. Inside, the fire pit in the central room looked large enough to roast several large reindeer at once. Leroy climbed down into the pit and built a fire using the flint and steel that Per had lent him. When the fire was burning brightly, he laid out more wood in a circle five feet across with an unburned space in the middle. In this space he put his food, knowing that it would be safe from roaches there.

Then he walked around the walls of the lodge, pouring out a thin trail of boric acid. Next he set the Roach Motels in strategic places around the main room, and finally he settled down to wait until the roaches came out. He'd seen them running away when he'd entered the gloomy lodge. Now that the fire lit the interior he could see them more clearly skittering around the walls. He waited until quite a few had moved to the center of the room, then jumped on them, howling at the top of his lungs and stamping over and over and over.

Wiglaff's villagers, passing by the lodge, heard his howls and reported them to Wiglaff. They heard the same howls night and day for seven days as Leroy stamped and stamped, pausing only to eat, sleep a little, and empty out the Roach Motels. Finally, a week after he had entered the lodge, he opened the main doors. Outside he found Wiglaff and all his people waiting.

"All over but the cleaning up," Leroy called.

The villagers cheered.

Wiglaff came forward, and Leroy led him into the lodge. He explained where he had kept his food and showed the king other ways to keep his food free of roaches. He also explained the purpose of the boric acid and told Wiglaff to see that it remained undisturbed. He gave Wiglaff the unopened bottles and replaced the empties in the paper bag.

"If you do these things," Leroy instructed, "keep the food safe and leave the boric acid, then the roaches won't ever come back."

"Never?" said Wiglaff, surprised.

"Never," Leroy insisted.

"That's powerful magic," said Per, who had followed his king into the lodge.

As they stepped to the double doors, Wiglaff commanded half his people to begin cleaning out the lodge and the other half to prepare a dinner fit for a hero. Turning to Leroy, he said, "What a feast we will have in your honor!"

Leroy waved to the villagers from the double doors and started down the stairs. Thinking of the feast to come, he missed his step, slid on a patch of ice, and landed on his head in the snow at the bottom of the lodge steps.

Leroy was cold. Snow was melting inside his collar, and he could hear someone calling. He opened his eyes. The gray sky above him was blocked by Mrs. Hansen's anxious face. She had seen him from her window and hurried down the back stairs.

"Leroy, honey, are you all right?"

"Uh, yeah sure, Mrs. Hansen, I'm fine. I've been in prehistoric Sweden." He started to tell her the whole story, but she cut him off.

"Honey, let's get you upstairs and get an ice pack on your head. We can call your mom, and you can tell her where you've been."

So Leroy wobbled up the stairs, and Mrs. Hansen took him into her apartment and sat him on the sofa with a bag of ice. She called his mother at work, and she came home to see if Leroy needed X rays.

All the time his mama poked at his head and looked in his eyes, Leroy tried to explain that he'd been to Sweden and saved the lodge and that he was Leroy Roachbane.

His mama said, "Yes, Leroy," and asked him to add six and nine. She finally decided that he probably hadn't killed himself, but he should spend the rest of the day in bed.

"But, Mama, the boric acid . . ." Leroy tried to explain.

"Don't worry about that, Leroy," said his mother. "I'll go outside and get it after you're in bed."

She did go downstairs and found the paper bag wet from the snow. Inside were the boric acid bottles. But they were all empty. There was no sign of the Roach Motels.

FACTORY

On his last night in the government-sponsored orphanage, John climbed to the top floor of the building to look out at the world. The city he lived in was huge. It stretched from horizon to horizon, and on an overcast night, like this one, the tallest buildings disappeared into the rain clouds that were swollen with the reflected orange of the streetlights below. Many blocks away, John could see the Gerwinks-Primary Factory, where he would begin work the next day. It was the largest of the factory buildings. It stretched for more than nine city blocks and was lit twenty-four hours a day by arc lights that were shocking white in contrast to the cheaper yellow street-lights that glowed on all sides. Work went on around the clock at Gerwinks-Primary. All employees were expected to be on call for emergency shifts. John watched what he could see of the bustling activity and wondered if he, too, would soon be hard at work in the middle of the nights. He wondered if there was any way to know, from the inside of the building, if the sun was shining or not.

There was a subtle change in the night sky overhead. The view of the world, and Gerwinks-Primary, was cut off by sheets of rain rolling down the windowpane. John went to bed.

The next morning he and seven other potential employees were waiting in the factory yard for the shift foreman. When the foreman arrived, he waved them into a small office without trying to compete with the noise of men and machines. Once inside the office, with the door closed, he introduced himself and explained the conditions of employment at G-P.

"You all will be on probation until you test out. Psych profiles have placed you in these jobs, but psych profiles and the government computers aren't infallible. People who can't get along in their jobs can expect to be fired. In the meantime, the factory will assign you a sleeping cubicle, and a food schedule, and will supply one uniform appropriate to your employment. Each of you will be assigned to a senior employee to be trained. John, you'll be with me. I know as much about the high cranes as anybody. Let's get started."

The foreman led them out onto the factory floor. One by

one, he dropped employees at their workstations until only John was left. Then he led the way to a ladder that climbed up one wall until it disappeared into a catwalk near the roof. John craned his head back to see what he could make of the machinery up there but didn't look long. It hurt his neck and made his stomach feel peculiar. He looked back down when the foreman began talking.

"I understand your psych profile says you enjoy working by yourself, and you're not afraid of heights. Normally you'd be trained by someone who works these cranes every day, but the last operator walked off the job without giving notice, and I can't spare one of the lower crane workers to break you in. Fortunately, I worked this crane and every other at Gerwinks. Used to be a high crane man before I was promoted. I'm pretty sure I remember the important stuff. We only use the big crane once or twice a day, so you should have plenty of time to figure out anything you need to know, and the rest of the shift will go easy on you for a bit. Any questions before we climb up?"

John had only one question. "That guy, the one that used to work the crane, he quit?" John had never heard of anyone quitting a job.

"Yeah, he said he got bored up there. Said he was lonely." The foreman shrugged.

Someone behind one of the surrounding machines called out, "Why didn't he just admit he was afraid of ghosts?"

The foreman looked in the unidentified workman's direction. John didn't hear him say anything, but the man at the machine turned quickly back to his work.

The foreman turned back to John. "Let's get started," he said, and began to climb the ladder.

* * *

The operation of the big crane was simple, but it responded slowly to instructions and so took some skill to operate. After the first few times up and down the ladder, the height ceased to bother John, and after the first week or so he was no longer winded and puffing when he finished his climb. This and one other thing seemed to prove the validity of his psych profile. John was entitled to one fifteen-minute coffee break every two hours, and a half-hour food break twice a day. But even after a month of building his muscles on the never-ending ladder, John couldn't get down from the crane and back up in less than eleven minutes. On coffee breaks, that left him four minutes to spend in the employee break room before he had to head back up to work. So he didn't climb down for his breaks and only rarely climbed down for the nineteen minutes he could grab at lunch. He didn't mind the lack of company, he preferred to be alone, but he missed the hot coffee. He went to the employee store to find a thermos. The shop girl was expecting him.

"Is it a thermos you're looking for?"

"Yes, it is, how did you know?"

"Well, I'd heard that there was a new man on the high crane, and every new man gets a thermos so he can take his breaks up top."

"Every one? Have you seen many people in this job?"

"Oh, yeah, three or four. Nobody lasts long. They claim that they get lonely up there, but if they weren't loners, they wouldn't have gotten the job in the first place. It's the ghosts." John wanted her to explain, but a look from her boss silenced her. John took his thermos and went back to work.

With a thermos and a boxed lunch, John was very happy. Once a week, he would check books out of the factory library and carry them in a pack up to the crane. During his fifteen-minute breaks, he would stretch out on the catwalk with a book and a cup of coffee, reading and sipping until a buzzer summoned him back to work. On the longer lunch breaks, he liked to climb to a particular alcove formed by crossing I beams and settle in for a longer read. So far above the factory floor, the noises of the individual machines and the shouts of the workers below were softened and provided a pleasant background. John felt he was in a world of his own.

For the first time, he had a little privacy to think his own thoughts. He didn't need to worry about what the Matron might discern from the expressions on his face. There was no one to bother him, no one to interrupt his reading as he paged through book after book.

"Excuse me. Excuse me." The voice repeated itself several times before John realized that high above the rest of the world someone was talking to him. He looked up. Standing with her hands on her hips and her head tilted forward was a girl with long dark hair. She was wearing a shapeless blue sweater and lighter blue pants. Her legs disappeared into the iron grille of the catwalk just above the ankles. John swallowed and gripped the covers of his book tightly. He continued staring at those feet, or anyway at the catwalk where the feet should be, until the girl said, "Excuse me," again in an exasperated voice. John wasn't sure how many times she'd said it already, but he suspected quite a few.

"Yes?" He couldn't think of anything else to say.

"You're sitting on my book. Could you move for a moment?"

"Uh, sure." John crabbed sideways about two feet. Away from the girl.

"Thank you," she said, "I don't like to reach through people in order to get things." She leaned forward and stuck out a hand. For just a second, John saw a book in that hand, and then she was gone.

That afternoon, John climbed down the ladder to eat his lunch in the employee break room. He looked around for a familiar face, and when he saw one he recognized, he went and sat down beside it. John had little experience in opening conversations, so he ate his lunch in silence. Only when he thought the other man might leave without saying anything at all did John begin.

"You, uh, you said something when I first started work, didn't you? Something about the guy who worked before me being afraid of ghosts."

"Oh," the man replied. "Are you the new guy on the high crane?"

John nodded.

"Yeah, I saw the guy come down from the crane one day, white as a sheet. The next day he didn't show up for work. The factory said he got bored and quit, but we all figured he'd seen a ghost."

A woman across the table heard the man and looked up. She smiled at John. "The factory does not believe in ghosts," she said. "No one is supposed to mention them." But she encouraged the man to tell the story. Other employees around them leaned closer. Ghost stories around the lunch table were too entertaining to be prevented by factory policy.

Many years before, the city had been smaller. At its outer

fringes were green spaces, public parks, and private estates. As the city grew, the green spaces disappeared, the parks were rezoned, and the estates were absorbed in lieu of taxes owed to the government. Only one open space remained.

"Before this factory stood on this piece of land, there was a preserve here," the machine operator began. "Owned by a family named Gerwinks. They had a big house on a hill in the middle of it and all around was trees and bushes and grass. There was a wall that kept the rest of the world out, and inside the wall there was supposed to be animals like rabbits and squirrels and things that hadn't been seen in the city for years. One day a bunch of businessmen came to see Old Man Gerwinks and said they wanted to buy the land. He said no. They kept offering more money, and he kept saying no. Well, lo and behold, one day Old Man Gerwinks gets smooshed by a truck right outside his own front gates. Too bad, bad brakes on the truck. Such a tragic accident.

"The businessmen go to Mrs. Gerwinks. They say how sorry they are about her husband and would she like to sell the property? Mrs. Gerwinks was tougher than they expected. She says no, just like the old man. So the businessmen went to the government and said that the land was going to waste. It shouldn't be allowed. If the land had a factory on it, the factory would make money and provide jobs, jobs people needed. So the government changed some laws and told Mrs. Gerwinks to sell.

"The old widow went to court. She said the land was special. She thought that anyone who wanted should be able to walk through the park. But the court told her that people didn't need grass and trees—they needed more buildings. The court told her she had to move. But the businessmen assured her that everyone would remember her husband because they would call the new factory the Gerwinks building.

"The judge gave the widow and her family until the end of the week to move out. She told the judge she intended to live and die in that house and nothing he said had changed her mind. She would live in it forever. She went home and locked the gates behind her.

"The bulldozers showed up on schedule Monday morning. Nobody had seen any sign that the family had moved out. The bulldozers rolled right through the gates and up the hill to the house, and that's where they found them." The man paused again in his monologue and took a sip of coffee.

"Found them?" John prompted, though he could guess the end of the story.

"All of them," the man said. "The whole family. The widow and her kids and her brother and his kids. She'd poisoned everybody who lived in the house, and they were all dead."

There was silence at the table. For a moment the noise of other employees in the lunchroom seemed very far away.

"Then what happened?" John asked.

The machine operator looked at John in surprise. He lifted his coffee cup and waved it at the walls around him. "What do you think happened, son? They buried those people and tore down that house and flattened the trees and stuck up this big old factory, and that's why we all have jobs and make money and aren't living somewhere in a doorway."

"But the ghosts come back," another employee insisted. "Every time there's been an accident with the machines somebody says they saw the widow Gerwinks come back to check on her property."

"My cousin works in the south factory, and she swears she saw two kids chasing a ball down an aisle," said another. "A week later a water pipe broke and the works were flooded for three days."

"But nobody admits to seeing the ghosts anymore," someone warned John. "People who do lose their jobs."

The machine operator put his coffee cup down and got to his feet. "Now," he said, "it is time to go back to those jobs, before the foreman comes looking for us."

Too late, John noticed the foreman sitting across the crowded room, looking at the cluster of employees. The group dissolved as each person hurried back to work, but the foreman's eyes remained on John. As John headed for the door, the foreman rose from his table and met him on the way.

"I'd like a word with you," he said, and walked with John back to the base of the ladder to the high crane. When they reached the ladder, the foreman took his arm.

"The factory doesn't like to hear too much talk about things it doesn't believe in. Contrary to what you may have heard, the factory has never found a single problem caused by ghosts. So if you meet any ectoplasmic spirits up there in the high crane, I suggest you be polite and they'll probably be polite right back. You're up there alone for fourteen hours a day, and you might find it's nice to have someone to talk to."

John started back up to work wondering if the foreman believed or didn't believe in the haunting. For the rest of the day and the rest of the week, John watched for another visitation, but as far as he could tell, he was alone above the factory floor. Each morning on his way in, the foreman picked him out of the rest of the shiftworkers and nodded a greeting.

It was ten days before John saw his ghost girl again. This time he saw her from the crane's cab as he floated by, ferrying a broken press to the repair shop. He couldn't stop, couldn't even slow down the crane. He just turned his head slowly and stared until she was hidden by the I beams of the alcove she haunted. She was floating eighteen inches above the catwalk, sitting with her feet stretched in front of her, reading a book. She never looked up.

After that, John saw her almost every day. Always in the same place, the alcove formed by crossing roof supports. Always she was reading. John couldn't make out what book. He no longer ate his lunch there, but he found excuses to send the crane by in the early afternoon. Rolling silently on the rails that crisscrossed the roof, he could watch for her from a safe distance. Once he saw her rising up through the catwalk as if she were climbing invisible stairs, holding a book open in front of her while she climbed. As much as he saw her, she never seemed to see him.

John thought, as he drifted along the roof, of the foreman's advice. Be polite. Maybe they'll be polite back. John had read more books since he started work at G-P than he had in his entire life. Reading the books was a luxury he would never grow tired of, but it would be nice to have someone to talk to, someone else who liked to read. When he had screwed up his courage, he walked over during a lunch break.

"Uh, hello."

The girl looked up in surprise. She put the book she was reading down beside her and it disappeared. John stood silent, tongue-tied by terror or shyness.

The girl continued to look up at him. "Did you want something?"

John swallowed and stammered, "Well, no. It's just that I've seen you here reading and I thought I'd, well, that it would, I mean, I just wanted to say hello. To be polite."

"That is very, very polite of you. Shall we introduce ourselves?"

"My name is John."

"My name is Edwina. It's nice to meet you, John." She smiled at him, and John felt the terror, or the shyness, whichever it was, break into pieces and disappear as if it had fallen through the catwalk at his feet. When she asked if there was something in particular he might like to talk about, now that they were introduced, John had an answer ready.

"What are you reading?"

It was a book by a man named John Muir. John had never heard of him, but Edwina said they were very interesting essays on nature. John was just promising to look them up in the library when the buzzer sounded, calling him back to work. Edwina told him to stop in and see her again the next day.

John looked for her during his next shift but didn't see her. It was the day after that that she was sitting in her usual place looking like a statue as well as a ghost. She moved only to flip the pages in her book.

She looked up and smiled when John said hello.

"I'm sorry I wasn't here yesterday after all. I was busy all day chasing dust balls with a mop. I've been here for hours today, though. Have you been busy or have you been ignoring me to teach me a lesson?"

"Neither," said John, "I've only seen you here for the last few minutes. I radioed down that I was going on break and came right over. You weren't here before."

"Strictly speaking," she said, "I'm not here now. At least I am in my here, but not your here."

"Exactly where are you," John collected up enough nerve to ask, "if you are not here?"

"Where is here, you mean?" she asked. "Here in deadland, in ghostdom, in limbo?"

"Is it, uh, heaven?" John asked, thinking back to his rudimentary instruction in religion.

"If it is," said the girl with a laugh, "it's everything it should be, but severely underpopulated. There's just us: Mother and Uncle Tim, and Todd and Eunice, and Richie and Alex and Angela and me. I never thought of heaven as being quite this exclusive. Is it your idea of heaven?"

"I don't know enough about it to say," said John, referring to his scant information on heaven, but the girl, Edwina, took him to mean her home.

"Sit down," she said, "and I'll tell you about it. You're the first nice ghost to come along in years and years."

Edwina described the house she lived in with her mother and uncle, her sister and sister's husband, her brother, Richie, and her cousins, Alex and Angela. The house she lived in was exactly the same as it had been just before the demolition team arrived. The days passed and the seasons changed, but year after year the house was exactly the same.

"And we have the mythical never-empty wallet of food

as well," Edwina explained. "As often as we take a cup of flour from its canister, a fresh cup takes its place. We have as much of everything now as we had when we started being dead."

John choked on his lunch. Edwina continued, "But we never have anything new, of course. Mother shopped very carefully, right up to the last, but even back then there were things you couldn't get easily. Chocolate, for instance. We've gone years and years without a taste of chocolate. I think the boys might have forgotten what it tastes like, but I still dream about it."

"Nothing ever changes? Not at all?"

"Oh, some things. Little things," said Edwina. "Mother has a stack of flower bulbs in the shed, and every year she plants them in a different pattern. We move the furniture around from time to time, but it always gets moved back eventually. Once there was a man who read poetry aloud, and I wrote it down. But that's the only new thing to come into our world since we died.

"And we never get any older. Richie and Alex will always be ten. My sister and Todd will always be newlyweds. Angela will always be two. And I will always be the only one with no one my own age to talk to."

"You have me to talk to," pointed out John.

Edwina smiled. "You aren't afraid to talk to a ghost?"

"Not at all." John realized the truth as he said it.

"Then I'll meet you here every day and you can tell me about all the books you have in your world that I don't have in mine. Do you read poetry?"

The room that Edwina saw when she sat and read was an attic. It was at the top of the house, which had stood on the top of a hill, and this was the only part of the house that reached as high as the roof of the factory. If he concentrated very hard, John found he could see the old chaise lounge that Edwina sat on, and in the mist he could see the room around her, the bare floorboards, and the curtains covering the window behind her. He saw them most clearly when Edwina read to him.

Edwina made a point of reading for a few minutes in the early afternoon when John took his breaks. He told her that John Muir's books weren't in the library. They'd been banned for many years because of their subversive content. Edwina didn't think they were subversive at all, and she read one of them aloud during John's breaks, to prove it. It took a week, partly because John interrupted over and over again to ask questions about the trees and animals that Muir described.

"Holy Cow," said Edwina when he asked her to describe a squirrel, "how can you not know what a squirrel looks like? Haven't you seen any animals at all? Next you'll tell me that there aren't any pigeons, and I won't believe you because I don't believe anything but nuclear war would get rid of pigeons."

"Pigeons?"

"They're a kind of bird."

"We have birds. Big black and gray things that leave white streaks on the statues."

"Those are pigeons," said Edwina, a little relieved to find something familiar left in the world.

"But we don't call them pigeons."

"What do you call them, then?"

"Just birds, there's only one kind."

So Edwina did her best to describe all the different birds

that she saw around her every day. There were sparrows and finches and doves. There were two different kinds of woodpeckers and a couple of titmice. There might be an owl living out in the woods. They thought they heard one from time to time, but they'd never seen it. Once she'd mentioned the woods, she had to describe those, too. They surrounded the house on all sides. Some parts were overgrown with brambles, and other parts, where the oldest trees grew, had a thick carpet of leaves on the ground and nothing else but the trunks of oaks and maples and the occasional evergreen. Edwina brought samples of different leaves to show John. Once she pulled the curtain away from the window and read him a poem about a man in a forest, and John strained his eyes to see the green trees outside, but he couldn't. All he saw was sunlight.

In return, John found books in the library that she had heard of but never read. She asked for poetry by a woman named Emily Dickinson, and Edna St. Vincent Millay. He read the poetry aloud and she copied it down. They both enjoyed the Dickinson, but didn't think much of Edna St. Vincent Millay.

"She has such a lovely name, though, doesn't she?" said Edwina.

"Have there been other people that you could see?" John asked one day.

"Other ghosts, you mean?" Edwina persisted in thinking of the people of John's world as ghosts. "After all, I feel solid to me," she had pointed out. "You're the ones who are all misty."

Yes, there were other ghosts. Edwina saw them from time

to time as they floated through her attic room. John was not the only one who favored the alcove formed by crossing I beams as a lunch spot. Occasionally ghosts did appear in other places.

"But remember, the rest of the house is below the roof of your factory but above the floor. Mother sees ghosts in the cellar whenever she goes down. And out in the meadow they appear three times a day, right on schedule. Hundreds of them sitting on benches and eating invisible food."

"Did any of them talk to you?"

"There was a man who talked to me quite a lot. He read me poetry, but he wouldn't read me any of Edna St. Vincent Millay. He said it wasn't worth the effort of carrying it up the ladder. I think he was right."

John was surprised by faint stirrings of jealousy. "What did he read instead?"

"I still have it all," said Edwina. "Wait while I get it." She rummaged through shadowy furniture, her arms disappearing to the elbow sometimes, and returned with a rumpled pile of papers. She read aloud poets and titles and snatches of poetry. Alexander Pope, John Keats, "The Eve of St. Agnes," Anne Bradstreet . . .

John asked what had happened to the provider of the poetry. Edwina told him that the man had been promoted after a few years to work on a different crane.

"He came back to visit several times, but then he said he was getting too busy, and I didn't see him again. I missed him when he was gone, or maybe I just missed his poetry. It was nice to have something new in the world, but I think it bothered him that he was growing older and I wasn't. He must have decided to spend his time with people in his own world."

* * *

John went down to the library the next day. He ignored the poetry section but selected carefully from a shelf of old detective novels.

They were highly successful. He read aloud from them over the next several weeks. Edwina's only complaint was that these were books that should be read while gorging on little chocolates filled with caramel, or maybe slightly sticky candy bars.

"Too bad," she said, "we haven't any chocolate at all. Not even to cook with."

"It's too bad mysteries are so much harder to copy down than poetry. I will miss them when you're gone."

"When I'm gone?" John hadn't thought about leaving, about being promoted or even transferred to another factory. He felt suddenly wretched and wished for the first time that he lived in a world like Edwina's where nothing ever changed.

"Edwina, how did you get the way you are? Did your mother really poison you?"

"Well. It was more than poison. I think she knew even during the trial that things wouldn't work out. She started collecting all kinds of food, and she did peculiar things. She poured flour and salt along the walls of the estate, and she painted every tree with paste. There was a terrific amount of work that had to be done. And she worried about Angela. She had a cold, and Mother said she couldn't guess which would be worse, to be a two-year-old with a cold forever or to live with a two-year-old with a cold forever. So she did everything she could to delay until Angela was better."

"Did you know?"

"You mean, during the last bit? No. We just ate dinner

together and went to bed. Everyone else slept through it but me. I woke up with a terrible headache and wobbled around until I fell out the window."

"You what?"

"Fell out the window. That one over there." She gestured to the curtain behind her. "I broke my back. My spine is all wobbly now, but it doesn't hurt."

"Will you really never change?"

"Never, never, never. You will get older and go away and forget all about me, and I will still be here. Lonely, with no one my own age to talk to and no chocolates." She pulled a sad face, and John laughed, even as he realized that he couldn't stand to grow older and be promoted and leave the high crane and Edwina forever.

"I will bring you chocolates," he said.

Edwina talked to her mother. Her mother climbed the stairs to Edwina's attic and talked to John for a long time. Just the two of them. Then John began collecting library books. He overcharged his card and anyone else's card he could borrow. He hid the books in secret places along the catwalk. He used his entire salary buying chocolates and obscure spices. And one day, during his lunch break, he drank his coffee laced with cyanide and lay down on the catwalk and listened to Edwina reading aloud a poem written in Greece more than two thousand years before John was born. It was really just the remaining pieces of a longer work, but Edwina had arranged the fragments to her liking and read them as if they were all part of a single poem.

> stop traveler and rest
> here in the shade of the trees

FACTORY

away from the dust of the road
near a graceful pavilion

Listen to the wind in the long leaves
the birds in the bushes
the water in the fountain
Sleep

as the shadows creep
as the sun

turns in the sky

Wake in the cool evening
when swallows seek their rest
Refreshed
as the moon rises.

At the end of John's breaktime, there was no sign of life in the high crane. The foreman climbed up.

The books were returned to the library. No one knew what to do with the boxes of chocolate and the cinnamon. The day-shift foreman took them home.

Several months later, the new crane operator pulled the foreman aside to tell him what he'd seen as he rolled by in his crane: two people, a young man and a woman, sitting on invisible furniture with their feet up, reading books and eating chocolates.

AUNT CHARLOTTE AND THE NGA PORTRAITS

I remember standing on the front steps of my great-aunt Charlotte's house. We were waiting for a cab, and my feet were cold. It was November, and I was wearing the kind of nice shoes that girls wore then with their best dresses. I thought that my feet would be too frozen to bend by the time the taxicab arrived, and I was considering clumping down the stairs like Frankenstein's monster, but I wasn't sure how Aunt Charlotte would take it. I'd been staying with her in her town house in Washington, D.C., for four gloomy days while my parents were away.

My mother had said her aunt Charlotte was very reserved, but she was sure that I would like her once we got to know each other. I wondered how long that would take. Aunt Charlotte averaged twenty-five words a day, and ten of those were "Would you like some breakfast?" and "Would you like some lunch?" After four days, I didn't know her any better than I had when she'd come to meet my train at Union Station. I had tried to fill in the silences and create a one-way conversation without much success. I wasn't sure that she had even noticed. It was only that morning that we had had our first real dialogue. She had invited me to join her that day for a trip to the National Gallery of Art. My mother had told me that Aunt Charlotte went to the NGA once a month without fail, and if I was invited, I should go, too. I wasn't much interested in paintings, but I said yes, I'd like to go, and went back upstairs to put on my best clothes.

When the cab finally arrived, I followed my aunt down the front steps with no Frankenstein imitations and climbed into the backseat beside her. It was an old cab. It smelled like cigarette smoke, and the vinyl on the seat was patched with squares of gray tape. The cabdriver wore a knit hat over his bushy hair. When he turned his head to ask where we wanted to go, all we could see were his hat and his hair and his nose. Aunt Charlotte said that we wanted to go to the National Gallery, and the cab pulled away from the curb with a lurch.

Aunt Charlotte looked over at me and folded her hands carefully in her lap. She said, "Well, Marguerite, you've told me a great deal about yourself in the last four days. I thought I'd tell you a little about myself and then we'd go see some friends of mine. How does that sound?"

I said that I thought it sounded fine, and after a moment
of lacing and unlacing her fingers, my aunt began her story.

I was just about your age the year that we went to
Ocracoke for Thanksgiving. My only brother was away at
college, so it was just my father, my mother, and myself.
Ocracoke is an island off the coast of North Carolina.
We had a beach house there. It's very beautiful in the
summer but doesn't have much to recommend it in
November. Still, my father wanted to go, so we did. My
mother was not pleased. She liked to go out in the
afternoon and visit her friends and drink tea and eat little
cakes and talk. None of her friends would be on
Ocracoke in November. They were all in Washington,
planning their next trips to London and Paris.

Unlike Mother, I was very pleased. Mother always took
me visiting with her in the afternoons, and I hated it. I
hated the tea and the little cakes and all the boring talk. I
dreamed of someday being old enough to stay home.

My aunt paused, but then continued.

Home was not really much better. My brother was so
much older than I was that I rarely saw him. I had a
governess to teach me, so I didn't go to school and I
didn't have any friends. I had never had friends, and I
didn't know that I was missing them. In fact, I'd have to
say I was something of a lump. I had a great many toys I
never played with and a number of books I never read.
Just about the only thing that I had any interest in was
fitting together jigsaw puzzles. . . .

When we went to Ocracoke, we took the train to Swan
Quarter and the ferry from there to the island. I was
surprised by how desolate it was in winter, with its skies

gray and the bright colors of the tourists' umbrellas gone.
Our beach house had to be opened up. It was damp and
chilled until the furnace was lit and the sea air dried out.
The other beach homes and the large resort hotel remained
shuttered and closed. The streets were empty. The few
winter visitors gathered for companionship at the smaller
resort hotel. The men sat in the bar. The woman spent their
afternoons sharing tea and a limited supply of conversation.

After a week, my mother declared herself wrung dry of
gossip and went back to Washington. I stayed with my
father. Once Mother was gone, I knew I would be
attending no more afternoon teas. I would have my days
to myself. Mother left me her gold watch with
instructions to see that my father ate lunch at twelve and
dinner at six, and except for those meals I was entirely
on my own.

I spent my days ruining the polish on my boots as I
scuffed along the sand beaches looking for seashells.
There was a hollow in the sand dunes, out of the wind,
where I would sit for hours, choosing the best of the
shells I had gathered. I was sitting there when I first met
Olga Weathers. It was a cloudy day, like most November
days. It was two-fifteen. At two-thirty I intended to return
to the house and ask my father for a dime for ice cream.
Every day I had asked, and every day he had shuffled
through his coat pocket until he had found the single
dime waiting there. There was, of course, nowhere to
buy ice cream on Ocracoke in November. The ice-cream
stand was firmly boarded up. Every night when he took
off his suit coat, I replaced the dime in its pocket, and
asked for it again the next day.

Aunt Charlotte broke off again and looked at me. The
cab had stopped in traffic at a red light. "You may someday

find that there is a certain contentment to be found in ritual, Marguerite." She went on with the story.

I was about to pile my chosen shells into my pockets and walk back into town when I saw a figure coming up the beach.

It was Olga Weathers. Never in my life, before or since, have I seen anyone like her. She was an enormous woman, probably six feet tall and as stout as the brawniest of the island's shrimpcatchers. She was wrapped in a man's overcoat that was unbuttoned down the front. Underneath, she had on a heavy brown dress that swept the sand as she waded through it. Gray streaks of hair streamed out of the bun on the top of her head. She lifted a hand to brush the hair out of her face, and as she did so, our eyes met. I smiled politely and then wished I'd been rude and looked away. She took my smile as an invitation and altered course to arrive beside me in my hollow. She settled next to me.

There is something awkward about adults who try to join children in their activities, but Olga was different. When she sank into the sand, it was as if she had taken possession of the whole beach and I was the one out of place.

"You are the little girl who's come to stay in the bungalow on Ocean Avenue?" she said.

I admitted that I was.

She introduced herself. "My house is near yours. I watched you putting a jigsaw puzzle together on your porch yesterday. You worked very quickly."

"It's an old puzzle," I explained. "I've put it together before."

"Is that fun? Putting together the same puzzle again?"

I shrugged. "It's something to do."

"You like puzzles."

I shrugged again. "They're something to do."

The woman was quiet for a moment. I checked my watch.

"You have somewhere to go?"

Surprised at myself, I explained about the imaginary ice-cream cone and the circadian dime. "It has been nine days. I want to keep asking every day until we go home. I bet myself that he won't notice."

"He sounds preoccupied," said Olga.

I shrugged.

Olga said, "Go ask for your dime. Then come and see me at my house." She heaved herself out of sand. "I live in the gray house with the pink trim. I have some puzzles that you might like." She swayed down the beach and disappeared between two sand dunes.

I collected the dime, then considered Olga Weathers's invitation. Finally I went and found my hat and skewered it to my head with a four-inch hatpin. I wore the hat because I knew that my mother never went visiting without one. The pin I thought would be a comfort in case of emergency. I crossed the street and knocked at the door of the house with the shell pink trim. When the door opened, I stepped into a living room at the bottom of the ocean. Heavy lace curtains admitted light that wavered back and forth across the greenish gray walls. The wood floors were polished to a light sand color, and on every flat surface were piled seashells of all descriptions. Somewhere someone was singing, or it might have been a radio playing. There was no one in the room besides myself. I looked around for Olga.

There was a hallway in front of me, and I followed it to the back of the house, where I found her on a sunporch that looked out over the salt marsh and the sand dunes. To my surprise, it was she who was singing as she pulled a comb through her hair. The bun was gone from the top of her head. Instead, her hair fell in waves of brown and gray down her back. With one motion, the comb swept from her forehead to her hair's distant ends.

I was captivated. My own hair was easily as long as Olga's, but it frizzed and knotted at every opportunity. When it was combed, it didn't float in perfect fans down to my shoulders.

When she saw me, out of the corner of her eye, Olga stopped singing. She wrapped her hair around one hand and pinned it up with a few deft movements. When it was back in its conservative wrapper, she turned to me.

"I thought you weren't coming. I had just about given up."

I smiled. "I had to get my hat."

Olga had a jigsaw puzzle that was a painting of waves. She and I spent that afternoon on her living room floor putting it together. While we pieced the edge together, we talked. I didn't read books, and I didn't know many people, and I hadn't learned anything of any interest from my governess, so I had not much to say, but Olga seemed happy to talk about jigsaw puzzles. She agreed that finishing wasn't the important part. It was the contentment that came with the placement of each individual piece. She asked me if I thought that this was true of different kinds of puzzles as well.

I asked, "What kinds of puzzles?" Jigsaws were all I knew.

"Like riddles," she said. "Like word problems. Do you like to solve word problems?"

I shook my head. "I don't know."

"There are puzzles everywhere," said Olga. "There are very simple kinds of puzzles, and there are kinds that grow more and more complicated. People are a puzzle. I like to piece together their actions in order to understand their thoughts." She looked at me. "Sometimes puzzles are so complicated you don't recognize them at first as puzzles."

Olga lifted her bulk off the floor with a ladylike grunt and went to pull a painting from behind an armchair. "This is a puzzle," she said. "This is very special, this painting. I looked for it for many years before I found it, and that was very satisfying, but," she sighed, "there is more to the puzzle that I haven't solved yet, and that is very upsetting."

It was an oil painting. Thousands of little dabs of paint had been put together to make a picture of a city. I wondered what was puzzling about it.

Olga looked thoughtfully at the painting and sighed. "I keep working on it." She slipped the painting back behind the armchair and returned to the jigsaw.

I spent every afternoon thereafter with Olga and her puzzles. She asked me riddles and produced brainteasers. We fitted together jigsaw puzzles, and we talked. Some days she suggested a walk on the beach. Whenever we topped the sand dunes and looked over the ocean for the first time, Olga would pause. She looked so sad that I finally asked what distressed her. She shrugged.

"You are growing a little more sharp-eyed, Charlotte," she said. "I am only wishing I could swim through the waves."

"It will be warm again soon," I said.

"It is not the cold that keeps me out of the water."

"Can you not swim?" I asked. I couldn't imagine someone living surrounded by ocean and being unable to swim.

"I used to swim," Olga explained, "like a fish. But then I changed." She waved a hand at her heavy body and shrugged. "With a body like this I would sink like a stone."

I looked her over and admitted to myself that Olga's bulk would be hard to propel through the water. I thought she must have been much thinner when she was younger.

"Do you go wading?" I asked. Lots of fat people did that.

"No, it only makes me sad to wade without swimming. But enough of that. We have puzzles still to be solved, and maybe someday I will swim again."

One afternoon I sat in Olga's living room waiting while she talked on the porch to a fisherman about the weather. I pulled out her painting in order to look at it more closely and wondered again what there was about it that was puzzling. I thought at first it was a picture of a river running through the middle of a city, but then I realized that it was a picture of Venice, where there are canals instead of streets. There was a bridge so steep that it had steps going up one side and coming down the other. There were people and shops all along the sides of the canal, and thin black boats, like canoes, crisscrossed the water. The boats were called gondolas, and I thought that the bridge must be the Rialto. I had read about it in my geography lessons. There were bright flags hanging from the bridge and the eaves of all of the buildings, and you could tell the sun was shining and the flags were blowing in the wind. When Olga came in, I asked her what the puzzle was.

"There is something hidden there, in Canaletto's painting," explained Olga. "It was put there by a very unpleasant man."

"You mean Canaletto?"

"No, not the artist, another man, who then hid the painting. So what I've been searching for has been doubly hidden."

"Why did he hide it?"

"He knew that it was very precious to me. He hoped that I would marry him in order to get it back."

"Wouldn't you?"

"No, even if I'd married him, he would have kept it and kept it and kept it, and I would never have been free. He thought I was helpless and had no choice, but I am not powerless, and I have a few friends. They helped me make a home on this island, and the people here pay me for what I can do."

"What do you mean?"

"Oh." Olga shrugged. "Foretell them the weather, find their fish, sometimes call their boats home when they are lost. Simple things."

I wasn't sure if she was joking or not. I asked, "What happened to the unpleasant man?"

"He was injured while hunting narwhals. The wound turned septic, and he died."

"Good," I said. If Olga said the man was bad, I believed her.

Olga lifted the picture behind the chair and sighed, "I just wish he had told me about the picture before he went off hunting narwhals."

"We leave tomorrow," I said to Olga as I stepped through her front doorway.

"So soon?" Olga asked vaguely. She was sitting in the dark of the afternoon in front of the Canaletto. She had her comb in her lap, but her hair was bound back in its bun. She sat on a small three-legged stool. The picture was propped on an easel, and all around were art books opened and closed right side up and upside down. Olga looked discouraged.

After a moment, she collected herself and asked if I would like a few cookies before starting a new puzzle. I said yes and followed her into the kitchen, where she burned herself twice boiling water for tea. We were supposed to work on a new jigsaw that afternoon, but I asked if she would like to go for a walk on the beach instead. Or maybe I should go home? I hated to lose my last day with her, but maybe she would prefer to be alone.

Olga put out one hand to my head and rubbed a thumb across my eyebrows. "It is that painting," she explained. "I have tried so many things without success. It makes me not very good company."

"Can't I help?" I asked, seeing a way to avoid spending my last afternoon by myself.

"I was going to ask you," said Olga, "but now you are going home, and I think it is too soon." She turned back to the tea.

"It isn't too soon," I said, not having any idea really of what she was talking about. "Let me try."

Olga thought while she poured the tea into cups. She handed one cup to me and took the other and a handful of cookies. "All right," she said. "We will try." She walked out of the kitchen and back toward the living room. With my tea and my own handful of cookies, I followed her.

Olga sat down on her three-legged stool, her bulk overflowing its sides, and waved for me to join her. The two of us faced the picture.

Olga took a last sip from her teacup and placed it on the seat of a nearby chair. One arm she wrapped around my waist. The other she lifted behind her head and pulled the pins from her hair. As her hair dropped, its smooth waves brushed across my bare arm.

"Look at the picture," said Olga. "What do you see?"

I looked, and I saw that each of the tiny figures in the painting was moving. The thin black boats crossed slowly from one side of the canal to the other. The larger boats drew closer or farther away. Crowds of people who were no more than scraps of color passed over the bridges, and on the waterfront more crowds hurried or dawdled or paused in conversation. As I watched, the picture grew clearer and clearer until I could make out individual faces and see the words printed on the prows of nearby boats.

"Can you see? Can you see?" whispered Olga, her voice strained with hope.

"They're moving," I whispered in turn. "Everyone is moving."

"Ah," Olga sighed in relief. "Then it is not too soon." I dragged my eyes away from the picture and looked at her instead. "It takes time for people to begin to see," Olga said. "Some never see. Those are the ones that take their boats out to sea and are wrecked because the skies

looked clear to them and they did not believe a
weathercaster's warnings. But even those who might
believe an old weathercaster don't see all at once. So
there are ways to teach them to open their eyes. Your
puzzles that are always new, the riddles and the word
games, have all shown you a new way to see. But it
takes time, and I did not think you had seen enough to
understand my picture."

"You're magic."

"Yes."

"You do cast spells for the people on the island."

"Yes."

"Wow."

Olga smiled.

"I thought when you said that something was hidden in
the picture, it was like one of those drawings with fifteen
things hidden in it that you were supposed to find."

"No," said Olga. "What I am seeking is more carefully
hidden than that. Somewhere in the picture is a place
that was not in Venice when Mister Canaletto painted it.
In that place is the thing that I have lost. But I cannot get
to it, even now."

"Why can't you?"

"Look carefully. The frame is very small, and I am very
stout. And see what lies across the bottom of the frame?
Water. Even if I could squeeze through the frame, I
would probably drown. If it is my only hope, I will
eventually risk it, but I thought that you might help me. If
you could."

"How?"

"You can fit through the frame. You can swim."

I still had my teacup in one hand. I took a sip from it and
thought before I answered. "Okay."

"Good girl," said Olga, and wrapped me in both arms
and squeezed until I almost dropped my tea. "Good,
good girl."

"Excuse me, lady." The cabdriver interrupted Aunt Charlotte's story. We were stopped at a red light behind a long
line of other cars. "There's some construction down there
near the museum. You mind if I take you the long way, up
Independence Avenue and back?"

"Oh," said Aunt Charlotte, "whatever you think best will
be fine."

I hunched forward on the seat until she began again.

Olga described the precious thing I was to look for in the
picture. A fur coat seemed a strange thing for Olga to
have sought all these years. Olga gave careful
instructions. She thought that if I found the coat, I could
take it without anyone to stop me, but if I ever was
frightened, I should come back.

"You are more important," she assured me, "than a
coat."

When I was ready, Olga began to sing. I reached out for
the lower edge of the picture frame, and it was as steady
and as firm as a stone banister. I hooked one foot over its
edge. I swooped my head through the frame and fell with
an ungainly splash into the smooth water of a canal. All
around me were boats filled with people, but no one
looked my way as I flapped and splattered through the
water. They showed no interest in me, a foreign girl
swimming through their canal in strange clothes. I was
invisible and inaudible to them as well. As I neared the
dock, I was nearly run down by several gondolas whose
gondoliers passed their poles over my head unaware of
my existence.

When I did reach the side of the canal, I realized a great difficulty. The water was more than two feet below the level of the stone street. I couldn't pull myself out. I looked back over my shoulder and could see the gold leaf picture frame floating four feet above the canal. If I couldn't even get myself onto the quayside, how was I ever going to get myself back up to the picture frame? Before I could panic, I heard a voice behind me say, "Here, turn around and give me your hand." The English words stood out from the babble of Italian.

I turned. A blonde-haired girl in a green coat bent down to take my hand. She braced herself and pulled, but not hard enough. My waterlogged clothes dragged me back. Before she'd had a chance to pull a second time, a boy arrived beside her. He was much more dramatically dressed, in a gold embroidered coat and a scarlet sash. He grabbed my other hand and pulled as well. Two others came to help. By the time I was out of the canal, a large puddle had spread across the stone pavement and my helpers were almost as wet as I was.

The four of them stood and looked at me, and I, with my hair dripping down my face and my clothes dripping onto the street, looked back at them. The first girl had a black flat-brimmed hat, like a sailor hat, that matched her coat. Beside her stood a boy, taller and probably older, in a fox red shirt a shade darker than his long brownish red hair. He, too, had a hat, but his was a deep black velvet rolled up around the edges. Beside him, and a little behind him, was another girl, dressed in a white dress with a black taffeta shawl across her shoulders. On her head was a peculiar collection of lace and ribbons that looked like a tiny wedding cake. She was pulling wet yellow silk gloves off her hands. The last of my helpers was a boy. He had no hat. His hair was trimmed very short and curled against his head. His clothes were far and away the most fancy, brightly colored and embroidered with gold. He looked like an illustration for a prince in a book of stories.

The first girl reached out a hand and said very formally, "I am Celeste." When I took her hand, intending to shake it, she sank into a curtsy. Beside her, the boy with the long hair bowed from the waist. "I am Antonio." The second girl also curtsied. She held her skirts out to the sides with both hands and whispered, "I am Caroline Howard." And the second boy stood up straight to announce, "I am Rannuccio."

I had no idea how to respond to introductions this formal. I thought that I should probably curtsy like the girls, but I didn't know how. The head bob I usually gave to ladies at my mother's tea parties wouldn't be enough. I stood paralyzed by shyness. Finally the girl called Celeste broke the tableau. She covered her mouth with both hands and stifled a burst of giggles.

"Oh," she laughed as she said, "you are so wet. You are like a cat pulled out of the well. A dog caught in a rainstorm." Her giggles were contagious. Antonio was the next to break down, then Rannuccio. I swept my soaking dress to one side and executed an exaggerated imitation of the girls' curtsies. Even Caroline smiled down into her silk gloves.

Celeste was the first to stop laughing. All her formality was gone. She took my hand and towed me toward the nearest bridge over the canal. "You are too wet to stand in the cold," she said. "Come to the other side of the canal where there is sun."

We climbed up the steps of the Rialto Bridge. Celeste kept tugging, but I paused to look over the edge at the top. I watched a gondola glide under me, before Celeste dragged me away. Once we reached a block of sunlit quay on the other side of the canal, she stopped.

"Here you will not be so cold."

Now that she had stopped, I had questions to ask.

Celeste told me that they all had been sent by Olga. Olga's magic had brought them to search Canaletto's Venice, but on their own they had not been able to find Olga's treasure.

"But we stayed to help you," said Celeste.

"Olga thought that you might like company," said Caroline.

"But where did you come from?" I wanted to ask why they were all dressed so strangely, but I thought it might be rude.

"From our frames," said Celeste. She was far and away the most talkative.

"You are . . . paintings?" I asked.

"Of course," said Rannuccio. "We are not Venetians." He said it with a certain amount of disdain that I didn't understand until later. Rannuccio was painted by a man in Florence. Antonio was also Italian. He was painted by Giovanni Boltraffio in Milan. Neither of them thought much of any city besides their own, although for the sake of politeness, Rannuccio said nothing of Milan and Antonio said only that he preferred Florence, of course, to Venice.

"But it is Venice we must search, and we should start soon," said Antonio. "But first you must get dry."

"Yes," said Celeste. "You must be dry or you will be cold."

I held my heavy skirts away from my legs. "If only I could shake myself like a dog," I said.

Caroline spoke up diffidently. "There is the clothing market. She could wear the gondolier pants and a sweater."

Rannuccio brought me the clothes. Then he and Antonio turned their backs while Caroline and Celeste helped me undo my buttons. I pulled on the pants, and dragged the sweater over my head. On a gondolier, the pants would have reached the knee; they covered me to the ankles. We used a scarf to tie them up. The sweater fell to my knees, and Caroline and Celeste rolled up the sleeves until they found my hands. As soon as my hands were free, I pulled Mother's gold watch out from underneath the sweater. It was round, like a man's pocket watch, and it hung on a gold chain around my neck. Until I changed my clothes, I had forgotten it was there. I should have taken it off before jumping in the water. I held it up to my ear and was reassured to hear it still ticking.

"Oh," said Celeste, "how pretty. It is like Papa's, only smaller."

Antonio and Rannuccio peeked over their shoulders, and when they saw that I was clothed again, they turned around. Neither of them had ever seen a watch or any mechanism so small and intricate. I showed them how the small door over the face popped open so that you could read the time. Then I very carefully opened the back so that they could watch the tiny gears winding around and around.

"How does it work?" Antonio asked.

I had to admit that I didn't know. "You wind this peg at the top and that makes the gears go around, but I don't know how."

"May I hold it?" Antonio asked. I pulled the chain over my head so that he could hold the watch. He stared into it, fascinated.

"What time does the watch tell?" asked Celeste.

Antonio thought a moment before answering, "Seven minutes until two o'clock."

"Do you know what that means?" Celeste asked. All but Antonio turned to look at her. "Lunchtime," she announced.

"Ah, no." Rannuccio slapped his hand against his forehead and groaned. 'She's hungry again."

"Of course I am," said Celeste. "We haven't eaten for hours. Aren't you hungry, Caro?" she turned to Caroline, who admitted that she was. Then she turned back to me.

"I'm hungry, too," I said.

"Back to the market!" Celeste clapped her hands with delight and skipped away. We all hurried after. Antonio handed me my watch, and I slung it back over my head, where it banged and swung against my sweater as I trotted along.

Like a row of obedient ducks, we followed Celeste along the canal. On either side of the water, the stone street was twenty or thirty feet wide. In most places it was filled with people going about their business, unaware of our existence. I nearly walked into someone who I thought would step out of my way. After that I was more careful to avoid other people on the street. It was harder than you might think to remember that they couldn't see me. And hard to keep Celeste and the others in view.

Ahead of me, Celeste began to sing as she walked, and it was easier to follow her voice. She led the way to an open plaza filled with stalls of fruit and vegetables.

Around the plaza were shops—everything that anyone could possibly want to eat. The five of us walked through the market and helped ourselves. Celeste took mainly pastries. She started a collection in the crook of one elbow. Rannuccio and Antonio each slipped a roasting chicken off racks where they turned above the coals. Caroline walked to the wine seller and casually selected a bottle from crates outside his door. Then we took the food we had collected to an empty bench beside the canal. I hesitated.

"Couldn't we pay somehow?" I asked.

The other four children looked at each other. "I'll show her," said Caroline, and led me to the back of the market, where side streets led deeper into the city. We walked to the opening and I looked into impenetrable gray mist. Next, Caroline led me to the wine seller and opened the door to the shop. On the other side was the same thick gray fog.

"There isn't anything there," said Caroline when I reached out a hand to touch it. "It's a painting. It only goes so far." She closed the door and led me back to the bench by the canal.

"You see?" Celeste asked when we returned. "It's a painting. When you go back, everything will be just exactly as it was before you came."

"Except that Olga's coat will not be here anymore," said Antonio as he licked the grease from the chicken off his fingers.

We ate our lunch and then we began our search. Celeste, Rannuccio, Antonio, and Caroline had already looked to see if anyone was wearing the coat. It was springtime in Canaletto's Venice, and anyone wearing a fur coat would be easy to find. They had looked in gondolas and other boats, as many as they could get into. We walked along the canal, looking in the market stalls and the shopwindows. We made our way down one side of the canal until the gray mist stopped us, then crossed a bridge and began to work our way up the other side. I stopped outside an arched doorway. The others turned back.

"What is it?" asked Rannuccio.

"I don't know." I looked around. There were two gondolas, pulled up at the side of the canal. They were tied to brightly striped posts like horses in stalls. The gondoliers were sitting on the edge of the street, with their feet dangling over the water. The street was made of large, uneven paving stones, and steps led up from it into the archway on my right. Under the arch was a chamber where people could stand out of the rain. At the back of it, in the shadows, was a glass door. It was the door that had caught my attention. It had glass panels on both sides, and I could see a wooden staircase with blue carpet beyond it.

I climbed up the steps to the archway and walked closer. Set in the door frame was a small brass plate with a button on it the size of my fingertip. It was an electric doorbell. I stepped back. At the top of the door was an address, and when I saw it, I knew that we had found what we were looking for. The address was 5478-B. Venice had certainly never contained an address like that.

I turned the knob and pushed open the door. Celeste, Antonio, Caroline, and Rannuccio came behind me, but when they reached the doorway, they found they could go no further.

"This is not the painting," said Antonio.

I went in alone.

I climbed the stairway. I turned once, then again. My friends were out of sight. There was a landing at the top of the stairs, and on the left a door. There seemed to be no lock. I tried the knob, and when it turned, I found a dim room filled with hunting trophies and dust. There were bookcases on the walls and above them the mounted heads of various animals. There were antelope and ibex and bongo. Above the empty fireplace was a huge sad-looking buffalo with its hair fallen out in patches. Here and there on the bookshelves were stuffed rabbits and gophers and birds. The windows were dirty. The room smelled musty and sad. I wrinkled my nose and looked around for Olga's coat. There was a table in front of the fireplace. It was empty except for a layer of dust and a rolled bundle wrapped in twine. I picked up the bundle and felt the softness of the fur. It was dark brown, and each individual hair was tipped with silver. I tugged at one end of the bundle until I saw the stitching in the collar, and then I was sure. It was Olga's coat. I tucked it under one arm, and I turned to go.

"What could you possibly want with that old thing?"

Sitting in a wing chair at the far end of the room was a harlequin dressed in turquoise and yellow and blue and red. He had no face, only a white porcelain carnival mask with ribbons hanging from its sides. Their bright colors were obscured by the same fine gray powder that coated everything in the room.

"Well?" he asked me.

"I'm taking it back to its owner," I said, and hurried toward the door.

"Why bother?" asked the harlequin, and lounged further back in his chair. He didn't seem anxious to stop me. I stopped myself.

"Why do her a favor?" he asked. "What has she done for you?"

I opened my mouth to answer, but the harlequin dismissed all my answers with a wave of his hand.

"Big deal. Some tea, cookies, a bunch of second-rate puzzles. She hasn't changed anything, you know." He leaned forward and planted his elbows on his knees. "If you go back, everything will be just the same. You'll get on the ferry tomorrow and go home to your dull life and your dull governess, and you still won't have any friends. You won't have anything to do all day but stick together boring puzzles and spend every afternoon with your mother at dull tea parties with dull ladies. Why would you go back to that? Why bother?"

What else could I do?

"Stay here," he suggested. "She can't make you climb back through the frame. She can't fit through to come after you herself. You have friends here, why not stay?" He was very persuasive. I wavered, thinking of the splendid day I had spent with my friends.

"No one will miss you," the harlequin pointed out. "No one will even notice that you are gone."

Olga would notice.

"Only because she wants the coat," the harlequin said. "That's all she cares about. She doesn't care about you."

But I knew that wasn't true. I was important. Olga had said so. She had said I was more important even than the coat.

The harlequin went on. "Stay," he said. "You'll never grow old," he said. "You can stay here forever and nothing will change."

It might have been a persuasive argument for an adult, but I wanted to grow up. I wanted to be old enough to tell my mother, no, I wouldn't go to her horrible teas. I thought of all the puzzles in the world without solutions. I suddenly realized that I wanted to go to college. It was an unusual thing for a girl to do, but I knew I could if I wanted. I would go to college and spend my whole life learning the solutions to puzzles.

"Stay," said the harlequin.

"No, thanks," I yelled as I threw myself at the door and jumped down the stairs three at a time. I burst out into the street and was lucky to miss knocking Celeste down. In a parade, we marched down the street and out to the Grand Canal. Rannuccio picked a gondola that he thought might pass under the picture frame, and we all piled in.

The boat passed the frame, but of course it did not stop. Very nimbly I had to throw myself up at the passing square with all my friends pushing and pushing until their hands could no longer reach.

"Good-bye! Good-bye!" I yelled as I teetered on the edge of the frame. With only one hand to balance by and the other wrapped around the coat I thought I was on my way back into the canal, but strong hands reached to pull me from the other side. I fell through the frame and landed in Olga's lap.

Later, after one last cup of tea and a long talk, we walked down to the beach together. At the waterline, Olga stopped to give me another fierce hug. "Good-bye, Charlotte. You will forget about me soon, but remember to keep looking for more puzzles." She kissed me on the forehead, then freed the last knot in the twine that wrapped the bundle and shook out a stiff dark fur coat as large as herself. As she walked into the water, she pushed her arms through its short sleeves and wrapped herself, clothes and all, in the fur. She fell forward into the next wave and was gone. When the crest of the wave had passed there was no sign of Olga. Only the brown head and shoulders of a seal bobbed in the water.

Somewhere behind us a car honked. We were stopped at a traffic light that had turned green. The cabdriver put the car into gear and hurried through the intersection. "Lady? Did you want to go to the East Building or the West Building?" he asked.

"West Building, please," said Aunt Charlotte.

The cab pulled around a corner and bounced across a cobblestone parking lot. It stopped in front of a pair of huge metal doors, and we got out. Aunt Charlotte went to pay the cabdriver, but he waved one hand out the window.

"No charge," he said. "Free ride. Best story I heard in my life, in my entire life." He drove away, his wheels squeaking on the cobblestones.

"Well," said Aunt Charlotte, looking after him, "I did think that it took a long time to get here." Her cheeks were pink, and she looked pleased.

"Was that the end of the story? Did you ever see Olga again?" I asked.

Aunt Charlotte took my hand, and we walked into the museum.

"No, that isn't quite the end of the story. I never did see Olga again, and it may surprise you to hear that I quite forgot about her for many years. Then one day, when I was home from college (I studied chemistry), I came to a fundraiser here at the museum. I brought my fiancé because I thought it would probably be very boring. During the speeches we slipped away and went to look at the paintings. Your great-uncle Emlin, you don't remember him, I suppose, was majoring in art history. He told me little snippets about the paintings we passed, until we reached this one."

My aunt had stopped at a small painting of a profile of a girl. Only her head and shoulders fit into the frame. She was wearing a dark coat and a hat with a wide flat brim that matched. Her blonde hair was long and straight. Her nose was tilted up, and her lips curved in a delighted smile.

"This," said my aunt, "is Celeste."

I read the plaque at the bottom of the picture carefully. It said "An Alsatian Girl by Jean-Jacques Henner." I looked up at my aunt.

"Yes, well," she said, "you can just imagine how surprised I was. It had never occurred to me that my friends must have had paintings of their own. All of my days with Olga came back in a rush. I dragged my fiancé through as much of the museum as was open, telling him the story as we went. He was able to suggest likely painters for each subject, but no others of my friends were here. Later, I paged through art book after art book until I found them all."

She tugged at my hand, and I followed her out of the gallery.

"I badgered the curators here at the National Gallery and donated pots of your great-great-grandfather's money so that this museum could acquire the portraits of each of my friends. I even found the Canaletto. You've seen it. It's the painting at the top of the stairs at home."

One by one, she showed me all of her friends. We walked across the main hall to look at Lady Caroline Howard painted by Sir Joshua Reynolds. The hat on her head did look like a small wedding cake. She was reaching out with one silk-gloved hand to brush the petals of the rosebush beside her.

Antonio was in the galleries at the other end of the museum. His nameplate said only "A Youth," but he had the chestnut hair that my aunt had described. Around the neck of his shirt was a thin collar embroidered with the same deep black as the velvet on his cap.

"See the tassels on his hat?" Aunt Charlotte asked. "I always forget those tassels until I see them again." They were tiny tassels, marked by just a dash of gold paint.

Rannuccio was not on display. My aunt led me by the hand through a door marked "Museum Officials Only." Behind it were cement corridors lit by bare lightbulbs. In a windowless office we found a man who was expecting us. He took us to a room filled floor to ceiling with racks of paintings. He slid one painting from the racks and carried it to an easel. Then he left us alone to admire Rannuccio in his fancy clothes.

Afterward, we went to the café. We sat in silence, Aunt Charlotte sipping her coffee while I drank my soda. Finally I had to ask, "Is it a true story, Aunt Charlotte?"

Aunt Charlotte looked at me without saying anything for a while. Then she said "I've told you my story. What you believe is up to you, Marguerite."

What you believe is up to you.

INSTEAD OF
THREE WISHES

Selene and the elf prince met on a Monday afternoon in New Duddleston when she had gone into town to run an errand for her mother. Mechemel was there to open a bank account. He had dressed carefully and anonymously for his trip in a conservative gray suit, a cream-colored shirt, a maroon tie. He was wearing a dark gray overcoat and carried a black leather briefcase. Selene hardly noticed him the first time she saw him.

He was standing on the traffic island in the middle of Route 237 when she went into Hopewell's Pharmacy and was still there when she came out again. She thought he must be cold on a November day with no hat and no gloves. He looked a little panicked out on the median by himself. The traffic light had changed. The walk sign reappeared, but Mechemel remained on the island, rooted to the concrete, with his face white and his pale hair blown up by the wind. Selene walked out to ask if he needed a hand.

"Young woman," he snapped, "I am perfectly capable of crossing a street on my own." Selene shrugged and turned to go, but the light had changed again and she, too, was stranded. While she waited for another chance to cross, the cars sped by. The breeze of their passing pushed Selene and the elf prince first forward, then back. It wasn't a comfortable sensation. When the walk sign reappeared, she was eager to get back to the sidewalk and catch her bus for home. A few steps into the crosswalk, she noticed that the elf prince still had not moved.

Rude old man, she thought, I should leave him here. But she stretched out a hand. Without looking at her, the elf prince put his arm around hers, and they walked to the curb together. Once they were up on the sidewalk, he snatched his arm away, as if it might catch fire.

"Well," he said with a sneer, "I suppose you expect a reward now."

Selene looked at the crosswalk. She looked at the old man. A nut, she thought. Nice suit, though.

"No, thank you," Selene said aloud. "Happy to oblige." She gave him the pleasant but impersonal smile she used on customers when she worked after school at the cafeteria.

"Of course you are." His voice dripped sarcasm, and Selene took a step back. "But I can't let you get away without one, can I?" When he fumbled in the inside pocket of his suit coat, Selene took several more steps back. He pulled out a wallet. From the wallet he extracted three small white cards and pushed them at Selene.

They looked like business cards. Instead of a printed name, a filigreed gold line wrapped itself in a design in the middle of each white rectangle.

"What are they?" Selene asked.

"Wishes," said the elf prince. "You've got three. Just make a wish and burn a card. It doesn't"—he looked her over with contempt—"require a college education."

"Thanks, but no, thanks," said Selene, and handed the cards back. She'd read about people who were offered three wishes by malevolent sprites. No matter what they wished, something terrible happened. She looked carefully at the man. Behind the nice suit and the tie, he was just as she thought a malevolent sprite might appear.

"What do you mean, 'Thanks, but no, thanks'?" The elf prince was irritated. "They are perfectly good wishes, I assure you. They're not cheap 'wish for a Popsicle' wishes, young woman. They are very high-quality. Here." He pushed them toward her. "Wish for anything. Go ahead."

"I wish for peace on earth," Selene said, and sneaked a look over her shoulder. Her bus was coming up the street but still two blocks away.

"That's not a thing!" snarled the elf prince. "That's an idea. That's a concept. I didn't say wish for a concept. I said a thing. A material object. Go on."

Selene stood her ground. "I'd rather not."

"Look," said the elf prince, "you get a reward for doing me a favor. I can't go around owing you one. What do you want?"

Selene could hear the bus rumbling up behind her. "Why

don't you pick something for me?" she asked. "Something you think is appropriate. How would that be?" The bus stopped beside her, and the doors sighed open.

"Well," said the elf prince with some asperity, "I can hardly think—"

"—Of something off the top of your head? I'm like that, too," said Selene. "Tell you what, when you think of something, you can send it to my house. It's easy to find. We live in the New Elegance Estates."

She hopped onto the bus. The doors closed behind her, and the elf prince was left standing on the sidewalk as the bus drove away.

Oh, she thought as she sat down, I wish I hadn't told him where we lived. I wish I hadn't.

Left behind, the elf prince was nonplussed. When he recovered, he propped his elegant briefcase on the top of a postal box and opened it wide enough to pull out a small Persian carpet, which he threw down on the sidewalk. He stepped onto it.

"Home," he snapped, and disappeared.

Selene and her mother lived in a housing development several miles beyond the suburbs of New Duddleston. The builder who had bought up the farm on the outskirts of the city had intended to build an entire community of different-size houses and apartment buildings. He had laid out the roads, and then paved all the driveways. By the time he began building the houses, he had run out of money. Only a few of the smaller ones had been finished when he went bankrupt, leaving the owners of those houses surrounded by vacant lots covered in weeds with driveways that led to no houses and roads that went nowhere.

Selene's mother was one of the owners. She had used her savings to buy the house and had hoped to take in a lodger to help with the mortgage payments, but so far no one had been interested in such a peculiar neighborhood. She and her daughter lived frugally on a monthly insurance check and waited for someone else to buy the land and build houses to go with all the driveways.

"Hello! I'm home!" Selene shouted as soon as she was in the door.

"I'm in the kitchen. Did you have a good day at school?" Her mother had her wheelchair pushed up to the kitchen table. In front of her was a plate of crumbs and one remaining half of a scone.

"Hey," said Selene, "I thought I told you to eat those up yesterday when they were still fresh."

Selene's mother smiled. "I ate as many as I could. And you know that I always think your scones are better the longer I wait."

"That's only because you're hungrier when you finally eat them. I bought the stuff to make more. And I got your prescription filled. Do you want a pill now?" The wrinkles around her mother's eyes showed that she was having a painful day.

"Yes, please, dear," she said. "I'm a little sore. Did you have any trouble getting the prescription filled?"

Selene was reminded of the peculiar man outside the pharmacy. "Not with the prescription," said Selene. "They know me at the pharmacy."

"But you did have a problem?"

"Not a problem, really. But I ran into a nutty old guy." Selene described her encounter with the elf prince. She provided a skillful caricature. "Still, I wish I hadn't told him where we lived."

"I wouldn't worry. He has probably forgotten all about you by now."

The next morning, as Selene was pulling on her coat before going to school, the doorbell rang. She opened the front door and found a shockingly green small man on the front step.

"Your gift," he said, "from Prince Mechemel of the Elf Realm of South Minney." And he swept a bow all the way down to his toes and waved it out across the stubbly crabgrass to the street. A golden coach and six black horses stood at the curb.

"Zowee," said Selene. "Is that for me?"

"Our master sends it to you and hopes that you will accept it as repayment of his debt to you."

"Oh." Selene paused. "Look," she said, "that's really nice of him, but could you . . . take it back? I really appreciate it and everything. It's very beautiful, but the coach would never fit in the garage, and I don't have anywhere to keep the horses. Tell him I said thank you, though." She carefully closed the door.

By the time she had walked to the living room window that overlooked the front yard, the leprechaun, the coach, and the horses were gone.

"Zow-ee," Selene said again, and went to tell her mother all about it.

"It's a good thing we don't have many neighbors," her mother said. "They'd wonder."

* * *

The next day the doorbell rang again. This time when Selene opened the door, there was an elegant woman with deep blue skin and dark green eyes. She was wrapped in a sea green cape that covered her all the way down to her toes and puddled there at her feet. In one thin, beautiful hand she held a set of keys on a silver key ring.

"Our master entreats you to accept these as repayment of his debt to you."

She held out the keys. Selene started to ask what they were for, when she caught sight of the mansion newly arrived on the lot across the street.

"Oh, my," she said. "Is that . . . ?"

"For you," said the blue woman with a happy smile. "Do you like it?"

"It is a beautiful house," said Selene.

"Palace, really," said the hamadryad. "It's got those gates in the front. I don't really remember if that makes it a palace or a château, exactly. I know that if it had a portcullis, it would be a castle, and it doesn't. But it does have those little turrets at the corners, so I think that means it's not a château."

Selene was silent.

"I'd definitely call it a palace," the hamadryad assured her. "You do like it?"

Selene said that she thought it was a lovely palace, she really liked the gold turrets at the corners, but she lived alone with her mother, and they could never use that much room.

The dryad looked so crestfallen that Selene rushed to say, "It's not that I don't like it. It's just that we're really very comfortable here."

"It's got central heating," the dryad said wistfully.

"We couldn't afford to pay the bill," Selene said sadly.

"And really lovely plumbing. Much nicer than we have back at the castle."

"I'm afraid not," said Selene. "But thank you, really. Please tell Mr.—His Highness that all this isn't necessary. He doesn't owe me anything."

She smiled at the dryad, and the dryad smiled sadly back and went away. The lovely white palace with the gold roof dissolved into mist and disappeared.

The next day Selene waited for the doorbell to ring. By the time she decided it wasn't going to, she had made herself late for school. On Thursday afternoons she worked in the school cafeteria baking rolls for school lunches. She didn't get off the bus until almost five-thirty and walked home through the pitch dark. She could see the lights in her house from a long way off.

As she went inside, her mother called from the living room. "Selene, do come meet the delightful young man who's come to marry you."

"Marry me?" She went into the living room. Her mother had her wheelchair pulled up to one side of the coffee table. On the other sat a young man, about Selene's age, in a fitted maroon velvet tunic that was held in place by a wide belt across his thighs. He wore dark green tights and leather slippers punched full of tiny cross-shaped holes. His cape was thrown over one shoulder and artistically draped on the sofa beside him. It was also maroon velvet but was imprinted with a leaf pattern. Green lace leaves in the same pattern trimmed its edges. In his lap was a soft conical hat with a twelve-inch blue feather curling above it.

The prince was very handsome, Selene had to admit. He had dark curly hair and very round blue eyes. He had the very cleft in his chin that is the prerequisite of fairy-tale princes.

He stood up and bowed from the waist. "A great pleasure to make your acquaintance," said the prince.

"It's nice to meet you, too," said Selene. "Did I hear that you're supposed to marry me?"

"Yes," said her mother. "It's what's-his-name's newest idea. He thought any girl would jump at the chance to marry a prince."

"That's the theory," said Selene. She turned back to the prince. "Could you," she said, "tell me a little about yourself?"

They spent a pleasant evening together, Selene, her mother, and Harold. Until her accident, Selene's mother had taught history at the high school. Since then, she had pursued her profession at home, sending Selene to the university library for enormous piles of books on the weekends. Now that she had a genuine fourteenth-century prince on hand, she had endless questions to ask.

Unfortunately, Harold couldn't answer them. He knew quite a bit about the clothes people had been wearing when he'd last been in the human world, but he didn't know anything about treaties or border disputes or religious schisms. All he could say was that he thought that a few heretics had been burned in his day, but he couldn't remember which kind.

"We had ministers to keep track of all those things," Harold explained lamely. "I'm sure that if they were here, they could answer all your questions." He looked around, as if he expected a prime minister or a chargé d'affaires to pop out from behind the sofa.

"What did princes do?" Selene asked.

"We gave treaties the authority of our names," Harold said grandly.

"How?"

"Well." The prince looked uncomfortable. "We signed them, you know, with our names."

They ended up discussing the elf prince's court. Selene asked about the plumbing. Her mother asked about the central heating. Then they asked about the elf prince. Harold was surprised to hear that Selene's impression of him had not been favorable.

"He's mostly really very nice," he insisted. "I once dropped a flagon of red wine in his reflecting pool and he wasn't angry at all." Harold did his best to convince them of Mechemel's kindness, his generosity, and his good humor. Selene was skeptical, but her mother pointed out that anyone who has recently had a fright can be forgiven a lapse in manners.

"I think the passing cars must have disturbed him," she said.

"Are elves really bothered by iron?" asked Selene.

"I don't know that it actually hurts them," said Harold, "but it does, you know, give them the willies."

"Yes, I see," said Selene's mother.

"Of course, automobiles give me the willies, too," admitted the prince. "Things didn't move so fast in my day."

Harold spent the night in the spare bedroom. They sent him back the next morning.

As she closed the door behind him, Selene's mother said, "He was a very nice young man."

"He was sweet," said Selene. "But what in the world would he have done if I'd married him? Gone out to look for a job?"

"Poor boy, can you picture him trying to get one?" Her mother laughed. "What are your qualifications? Well, I look good in velvet and . . ."

"Can't read or write . . ."

"Can't type, can't drive, don't know what electricity is, never heard of a vacuum cleaner."

"He couldn't buy groceries, cook dinner, or pay bills."

"If you wrote out the checks, he could sign his name," Selene's mother reminded her.

"Oh, of course," said Selene, "he would have *ministers* to take care of all that." She added, "He'd do okay if he just came with a pot of gold."

"Oh, no," said her mother. "That's *leprechauns*."

Selene was late for school again. As she went out the door, she said, "This is the third gift we've rejected. Do you think His Highness the elf prince of wherever will give up?"

Mechemel wasn't giving up. He was getting out the big guns, going to the experts, checking with an authority on humans. He went to talk to his mother. She had a room at the top of the castle with windows on all four walls so that she could lie in bed and look out at the forest. She was old and a little frail, and she didn't get around much, so she passed her time keeping an eye on daily activities in the forest and watching television.

Mechemel climbed up the stairs to her tower. He sat beside her bed and twiddled his thumbs while he explained his difficulty. After a while he grew suspicious of her silence and looked up in outrage.

"You're laughing at me!"

"Mechemel"—his mother's laugh was a lovely sound—"this is the most foolish thing that I have ever heard in my life. I warned you about how fast those iron contraptions can go."

"It's your fault," said Mechemel. "You're the one who wanted to keep your gold in a bank. Who ever heard of fairy gold in a safe-deposit box? Much less a checking account?"

"I know, dear." She smiled apologetically. "But so many of these mail-order companies want to be paid by check or money order, and the sprites were complaining about the lines at the post office. I thought you'd send a leprechaun."

"Leprechauns are unreliable," grumped her son. "They only have to meet one sharp character, and they hand over everything."

"Yes," admitted the fairy queen, "but surely you could have sent a hamadryad, or even one of those human princes that are always hanging around."

"Hamadryads are even worse than leprechauns, and the princes, well . . ." He smiled ruefully at last. "There's no point pretending that any of them were gifted with brains."

"And here you are fussed because the mortal girl thought the same thing. Stop sulking and admit that this is funny."

Mechemel stiffened and then stifled a snort. "You should have seen her face when I pulled out the wishes. She looked afraid for her life."

"She probably was, poor thing."

"What did she think I would do, turn her into a frog?"

"She probably thought that you were a homicidal maniac."

"A what?"

"You don't watch enough television, Mechemel. It's one

■ 84 ■

of those humans that go around murdering other humans for no good reason." She waved one hand at the television set on a stand beside the bed. It stood on a stand of crystal and carefully wrought gold. Its cord ran across the floor and out one window, where it dropped to the ground and was wired directly into one of Ontario Hydroelectric's cross-country power cables.

"I don't understand how you can stand to watch that."

"Oh, it's amusing sometimes. It's so terribly dull, since the humans have stopped coming to court. There's never anyone new to talk to. Watching them talk to each other is the next best thing."

"You should go out more."

The elf queen slipped deeper into her feather pillows. "It's too much trouble. Things have changed too much in the last hundred years. Besides," she added slyly, "look what happened to you."

"It's all very well to snicker about it. The longer I owe her a favor, the more in debt I am. So . . ."

"So what?"

"So tell me what will make her happy."

"I haven't a clue."

"But you're supposed to know!" He threw up his hands. "And stop laughing!"

His mother reached out a hand to pat him on the knee. "Don't worry," she said. "You find out a little more about her, and then we'll think of something."

On Saturday, Selene was out in the front yard, sawing at a dead tree, when the elf prince arrived. The tree had been the builder's one attempt to fulfill a clause in the contract that said "fully landscaped." Stuck into ground packed hard by bulldozers and surrounded by weeds, the little tree had given up immediately and died. Selene didn't mind the weeds—many of them were pretty—but the brittle branches of the dead tree depressed her, so she was cutting it down.

She looked up from her work and realized a man was watching her from the sidewalk. "Are you the next silly idea of that ridiculous elf?"

"No," said Mechemel, and didn't say anything else.

Selene was terribly embarrassed. She looked from her saw to the tree and back to Mechemel.

"Yes," he said, "do stop dismembering that poor bush and invite me in."

"It's a tree, actually."

"Bush," said Mechemel. "*Salix bebbiana*. Or it was. All it is now is dead."

He moved past Selene toward the ramp that led to the front door. "Fortunately uninhabited," he said as he went.

Still carrying the saw, Selene followed him up the ramp and into the house. He waited in the hall while she went to fetch her mother. He looked startled when Selene rolled her in, but collected himself quickly.

"I understand," he said, "that you are willing to take a lodger?"

Selene's mother asked him for references, and he provided them. He told them that he was a visiting professor at the local university.

"Waterloo or Wilfred Laurier?" Selene's mother asked.

"Uh, Waterloo."

"Lovely, perhaps we know the same people. You said you were in the history department?"

Mechemel saw that he was on dangerous ground and retreated rapidly. He was new there; he didn't know anyone; he wouldn't actually be teaching in the department, just doing research.

"Oh," said Selene's mother, disappointed. "Well, still. I'm sure it will be very nice to have you as a lodger. Did you say that you wanted to take your meals here?" she asked hesitantly.

Mechemel shuddered. "No, thank you," he said.

So Mechemel moved in. Selene and her mother wondered about their new lodger. He came with very little luggage, just the one suitcase. He was always home at dinnertime, but he never seemed to eat. Selene cooked her mother dinner, and the two of them ate at the kitchen table, wondering what Mechemel was doing in his room.

"Maybe he lives on store-bought cookies and soda," said Selene.

"It would be warm soda," her mother pointed out. "He doesn't have a fridge." They didn't see the leprechauns skipping up to the spare bedroom window, carrying trays of covered dishes. Mechemel was willing to sacrifice in order to get his debt paid off, but he was not going to eat whatever humans called food. Before he'd left the castle, his mother had told him dire stories about microwaves and things called burritos.

Mechemel had been staying with Selene and her mother for a week before Selene did any baking. On Friday, Mechemel's rent payment made it possible to buy an extra dozen eggs, baking chocolate, and five pounds of extra-fine cake flour. In the evening, she read through her collection of secondhand cookbooks and decided that she wanted to try a brittle chocolate crème de menthe gâteau.

"It sounds wonderful," said her mother. "Do we have crème de menthe?"

"Somebody brought some to the Christmas party last year. I think it's still in the closet over the oven."

"Now that we are rolling in dough, so to speak, will you not be making any more scones?" In the past, Selene's baking had been limited to a weekly batch of scones because their ingredients were affordable.

"Oh, I'll make those first thing in the morning, then try the cake," said Selen, and she got up early on Saturday in order to have the scones ready for her mother's breakfast. Mechemel woke to the aroma of buttermilk currant scones baking in the oven. He got out of his uncomfortable narrow bed and into his clothes before being pulled irresistibly into the kitchen. Selene was measuring out ingredients for her cake with the precision of a chemist; her mother was having a cup of coffee. Mechemel sniffed, appreciatively.

"Are those scones?" he asked. He suffered from an elfin addiction to sweet things.

"Yes," said Selene, without turning around. There was only half an inch of crème de menthe left in the bottle, and she was looking through the recipe to see if it was enough.

"May I have one?"

"Of course." Selene looked around and smiled at him, before turning back to the recipe. It was not the impersonal smile that she used on customers; it was a real one that she reserved for people she thought she might like.

Mechemel's eyebrows went up in astonishment. He remembered that Harold had said she had a smile that would make flowers bloom early, but he had assumed that Harold was exaggerating, as Harold always did. Mechemel sat down at the table. While Selene's mother watched in amusement, he ate the entire plate of scones. The only one left was the one in Selene's mother's hand.

When Selene was done measuring out the crème de menthe, she looked at the plate, empty of all but crumbs. "You ate them *all*?"

Embarrassment colored Mechemel's face deep pink. "I am terribly sorry. I don't know what came over me. . . . I, um . . . It's been some time," he explained, "since I had scones. And these really are, were," he corrected himself, "delicious."

He grew still pinker when Selene laughed. "It's okay. I can make more," she said, "but see if I offer you any cake."

"You're making a cake?" Mechemel said with delight, then backtracked hastily. "Well, no, no, I certainly wouldn't trouble you for any." He stood up from the table and tried not to look disappointed.

Selene's mother reached up to pat him on the arm. "No, sit down," she said. "Selene was only teasing."

The elf prince looked at her in surprise. He wasn't used to being teased, and no one but his mother had ever patted him on the arm.

So Mechemel sat at the kitchen table and talked to Selene's mother while Selene made her brittle chocolate crème de menthe gâteau. Selene's mother told him their version of the week's events and ended up saying, "In fact, if you had been a present from the elf prince, you would have been perfect."

Mechemel winced. If he had known, he could have sent them a real lodger. It was too late now.

Selene's mother asked Mechemel about his research project, and he made up answers as well as he could. He gathered that Selene's mother was writing a dissertation on something called the Battle of Hastings. He drew a strange look when he raised one eyebrow and said, "Which one was that?"

"Surely you know the Battle of Hastings. When the English lost to the Norman invaders?"

"Oh, yes, of course. How silly of me, yes. A friend of mine was there." He saw another startled look forming and realized his error. "Last year, at the site, not at the battle itself, of course." After that he thought he had better excuse himself. He went back to his room and didn't come out until the cake was ready. He ate half of it.

On Sunday, Selene made another batch of scones for herself and her mother and one batch for Mechemel to eat all by himself. On Monday, he came home in the evening with a bag of groceries and a jar of cloudberry jam. He said that he didn't think it was fair that they spend all his rent money feeding him.

"The jam is from my mother's pantry."

"Oh, does your mother live near here?"

"Not far," he responded, "as the crow flies."

Every week, Mechemel would bring home a bag of ingredients for scones and other delicacies, and on Saturdays, Selene would bake, experimenting with every recipe in her worn-out cookbooks. On weekdays, when Selene and her mother thought he was going to sit in the library at the University of Waterloo, Mechemel went home to talk with his mother. He described Selene's sugary concoctions in detail and related his conversations with Selene's mother. Then he and his mother tried to pick a gift that would please Selene. His mother suggested a cubic zirconium tennis bracelet that she had seen advertised on the shopping channel.

"She doesn't wear any jewelry. She'd probably sell it to buy cake flour. As nearly as I can tell, baking is the one thing she enjoys."

"Buy her five hundred pounds of cake flour."

"I can't. Every time I give her that sort of thing, she makes more cakes and scones and I eat them."

"Well, I don't know which I envy more, your never-ending supply of sweets or the company of that girl's mother. She seems quite clever."

"She is."

"We haven't had a clever person here in years." Mechemel's mother sighed, and Mechemel promised that when he had taken care of his obligation to Selene, he'd try to find something that would amuse her, maybe a videocassette recorder.

He was always back at the house in New Elegance Estates in the late afternoon to share a cup of tea and a long talk with Selene's mother. While they talked, they ate Selene's scones. They discussed history, more often than not; it was Selene's mother's passion. She was particularly interested in Canadian history, and Mechemel, who had lived through a good part of it, was able to provide eyewitness reports of several events. He, of course, lied about the source of his information.

So a little of Selene's mother's loneliness was relieved, and a little of Mechemel's mother's boredom, but Mechemel got no closer to finding a gift to repay Selene. With each passing day, he was more determined to choose a gift without parallel. Money was too easy. He wanted something better.

In the springtime, New Elegance Estates looked as good as they ever did. All the weeds were blooming. The empty streets were washed clean by nightly rains. Mechemel walked home one evening, avoiding puddles, carrying his bag of groceries. He heard footsteps pounding behind him and turned to wait for Selene. Behind her, the number seventeen bus pulled away.

Selene didn't bother to evade the puddles. As she ran, she stamped heavily into each one in her path, spraying water in circles across the pavement. She slowed down before she reached Mechemel, but several especially motivated droplets landed on his shoes. He leaned to look at them over the top of the grocery bag, then looked at Selene with his eyebrows raised.

"Heavens," she said, "will you melt?"

He watched the drops evaporate before he answered dryly, "I think I'm safe. Did you have a good day at school?" He made a hook with his elbow, and she caught her arm through it. They walked shoulder to shoulder toward home.

"Good enough. Only sixteen more days to go." When they got to the front yard, Mechemel pointed with his chin.

"Your bush has rejuvenated."

Selene was stunned. She had never finished the job that she'd started the day Mechemel arrived. All winter, the tree had stood with its trunk sawed halfway through. Now that the warm weather had come, tiny shoots of green had sprung from the bark below the cut.

"I think you'll find that you can cut away the dead part and those green shoots will grow up into a very pretty bush."

"You said it was a bush before, what did you call it?"

"*Salix bebbiana*. It's one of the diamond-barked willows."

"Goodness, you know a lot."

"Not everything," said Mechemel.

That was the day that the letter came. Selene found it in the mailbox at the top of the ramp to the front door. She dumped her schoolbooks down in the front hall and sat beside them while she read it. Mechemel watched her face grow pink with pleasure and then fade with disappointment.

"What is it?" he asked.

"Oh, it's a letter from the Boston School of Culinary Arts."

"Yes?"

"I sent them my scones by overnight mail. As a sample of my work. They liked my scones, and they say I can enroll in their school." She looked up at Mechemel. "They are very exclusive. It's an honor just to be invited to enroll, especially for the pastry program. Listen," and she read aloud from the letter. " 'We thank you for your application. The judges enjoyed your scones and feel that although their charm is rough, you may have talent worthy of cultivation.' "

"Sounds very pompous," said Mechemel.

"They are, but famous, too."

"Did you want to go study there?"

"Lots."

"Then why aren't you more pleased?"

"No money," said Selene.

"Ah," said Mechemel, suddenly understanding.

"Besides," said Selene as she folded up the letter and put it away, "there's Mother. She'd hate to move to Boston. And I couldn't leave her here on her own, so it's no go either way."

"What will you do instead?"

"Probably take the job they've offered me at the school

cafeteria. It's full-time." She collected her books and left Mechemel standing in the front hall.

After a while, he put his bag of groceries down and went back out the door to visit his mother.

The next day was Thursday. Selene came home late, but the sunset was not yet over when she closed the front door behind her.

"Selene," her mother called, "come into the living room."

Selene went to the doorway. "Only fifteen days left," she said to her mother, who had her wheelchair pulled up to the coffee table. Mechemel was sitting on the couch next to her. "What's up?" Selene wanted to know.

"Remember that elf prince?" said her mother.

"Oh, no," said Selene. "He hasn't resurfaced, has he?"

"He has," said Mechemel.

What now? Selene almost said aloud, but thought better of it. She looked at Mechemel and blushed.

"He's been slow," said her mother, "but he has finally selected a present for you." Mechemel handed Selene an envelope. Inside, a piece of parchment, much adorned with ribbons and seals, informed her that she was the recipient of a centennial scholarship awarded for excellence in the Very Fine Art of Scone Making and that the Mechemel Foundation would pay the tuition and board at the School of Culinary Excellence of her choice, so long as it subscribed to the high standards of the foundation.

"But I told you—" Selene directed a fierce look at Mechemel.

"And," her mother interrupted her, "while you are away at school, Mechemel's mother has most graciously invited me to stay with her. For as long as is necessary to complete your education," she emphasized.

"With her?"

"And myself," said Mechemel.

"Yes," said Selene's mother with a smile, "I'll be able to give Harold your regards."

"Zowee."

So Mechemel arranged for a dryad to move into the willow in the front yard and keep an eye on the house. Selene went to Boston, and her mother became great friends with the elf queen. In the evening, they sometimes watched television together, but mostly they talked. Mechemel sometimes stopped in, and the three of them discussed the Meech Lake Accord and the French and Indian War. In the summer, Selene came to visit as well and demonstrated what she'd learned in school: cherry coulis, blancmange, clafoutis, mille-feuille, and puff pastry with fresh strawberries picked in the forest by the sprites. And every afternoon, she made a fresh batch of scones for tea.

THE NIGHTMARE

Summer vacation had long since trailed off into empty days and boredom. Twice that afternoon the boys had been chased away from the bus stop, where they liked to hang out, making boasts and idle plans. The manager of Orly's deli stepped out of his doorway ready to chase them away a third time; the bus stop benches were for people who used the buses, not for a bunch of near adolescents who had nothing to do with their time but make trouble.

With their hands in their pockets and their chins in the

air, the boys prepared to move on, pretending to themselves that it was their decision, not somebody's pushing, that was making them go, when a bus pulled up and squeezed out a puddle of tired commuters.

It was Kevin's idea to follow the dowdy old woman. He gestured to his friends, and they fell in behind him. Walking tough with their hands still in their pockets and their shoulders rolled forward, they followed her up the sidewalk until she turned off on Fifty-fourth Street. They turned the corner as well and pulled a little closer. The old woman glanced back. She wasn't really old, not much older than Kevin's mother. Her skin was smooth, but the hair that pushed out from under her knit hat was streaked with gray. Her dress was gray, as well as the coat she wore. She was dingy and drab and not very interesting. Kevin wasn't sure why he had chosen to follow her.

The woman turned left at Blackstone Avenue. When she looked back again, she could no longer pretend that coincidence kept her and the boys on a shared path. She put her head down and walked faster.

Kevin, stepping along in front of his friends, matched her speed, feeling proud of the anxiety a group of seventh graders could inspire. He and his friends had never done anything like this. Although they'd bullied the younger kids at school, they'd never before intimidated an adult. He thought it was a turning point. No doubt when school started in a few days, Kevin and his friends would be able to make even the high-school kids sit up and take notice. Absorbed in his daydreams of power, he didn't notice that the woman ahead of him had stopped until he almost ran into her. Startled, he stepped back and bumped the boy behind him.

"Well, what do you want from me?" the woman snapped with a ferocity that hadn't been there only a moment before.

Kevin felt the blood rushing to his face as his daydreams broke up. He felt foolish and was afraid to be laughed at by his friends. He swept his shattered dignity together and said in a cocky voice, "I want whatever you've got." Behind him, his friends stirred nervously. They had been teasing the old woman for fun, and Kevin was pushing things further than they were willing to go. Their hesitation drove him on.

"Come on, lady, what have you got?"

"This is what I've *got* and you can have it." She pulled her hand from her coat pocket and threw something at him. He cupped his hands in front of his chest and caught it there. Something that felt like a blob of Jell-O smacked into his palms, but when he looked, his hands were empty. He looked up again as the woman disappeared into a nearby apartment building. The lock on the door clicked shut behind her.

Kevin looked down at the sidewalk to see if he had dropped whatever it was. He saw nothing. He shrugged. "Come on, let's go up to Walgreen's. Get some candy and stuff."

That night, Kevin lay in bed listening to the television that was on in the living room. It was a murder mystery that his parents were watching. Listening to the dialogue, Kevin tried to visualize the story in his head. The lady had told everyone that she knew who the killer was, even though she didn't. She just guessed. But she thought that if she pretended she had evidence, the killer would come after her and then she would have proof to take to the police. Now she was alone in the house at night and the killer was getting closer. There were long periods of silence broken by little crackling noises and suspense music. Kevin figured the killer was lurking in the bushes outside the house. The lady in the house thought she was safe, but she wasn't. The killer was getting closer. He crept up the steps of the back porch. Kevin rolled over on his side. The killer started checking the windows to see which one was open. The killer stepped from the back porch to the ledge of Kevin's window, but it was safely locked. The killer rattled the frame just to be sure. Then he stepped back onto the porch. Kevin could hear him checking the lock on the kitchen door, turning the knob, and bumping the door back and forth. Kevin wanted to call for help, but he was alone. After a few minutes, the bumping stopped. Kevin relaxed.

Then he heard the creaking of steps in the stairwell. Somehow the killer had gotten through the front door of the apartment building. He was climbing the stairs to Kevin's apartment. Terrified, Kevin realized that his front door wasn't locked. He tried to jump out of bed and run down the hall to the door, but he couldn't move. Lying there in the dark, he heard the front door opening. He heard the footsteps in the hall, getting closer and closer. The killer was coming. He was bringing something horrible with him. He crept closer with each step until Kevin knew that the killer stood in the dark right outside his own bedroom door. Kevin couldn't see, but he knew the door was opening.

Kevin threw the covers off and jumped out of bed, ready to run, but there was no need. It was morning. The sun was coming in his window. The door to his bedroom was still closed. It had all been a nightmare. With his knees still shaking, Kevin got back in bed and huddled under the blankets.

The next night, giant snakes slid out of the ground all around the apartment building. They slithered through the dark, up the fire escapes, and across the back porch. They curled on the window ledges and pressed their cold bodies against the glass. Each one carried a mirror in its mouth that clicked and scratched against the window.

In the morning Kevin couldn't convince himself that the snakes weren't still there. He wouldn't leave the apartment until his sister had been outside and down the stairs without being eaten. By the time he found his friends at the basketball court, they had already chosen teams, and there was no room for Kevin to play.

After the third nightmare, Kevin was desperately happy to see the morning. He set off to the schoolyard, tired but cocksure, confident that the power he had wielded as a sixth grader in an elementary school would be waiting for him as a seventh grader in junior high. His confidence disappeared with his lunch money when kids from the high-school side of the building shook him down in the schoolyard.

Kevin had never been in a school where students changed classes with each subject. He didn't share a homeroom with his friends; he had no one to remind him that he was cool and tough and didn't need to be intimidated by a complicated schedule and unfamiliar teachers. He had to bully a couple of kids out of their small change to make himself feel better and get enough money for lunch.

Lunch should have been a pleasure. Kevin had never known a school cafeteria to sell ice-cream sandwiches. They were all he had money for, but they were all he wanted. He never saw the foot that snaked out and tripped him as he made his way to the junior-high side of the lunchroom. His lunch tray flew into the air as he stumbled to his knees. The whole lunchroom laughed. Somebody stepped on his sandwich.

In the afternoon he got lost and ended up in the high-school side of the school, where he was chased by the same group that had taken his lunch money in the schoolyard.

"Hey, Kevin," they called down the hallway, "we heard you're really tough."

"We heard you were the big man of the sixth grade."

"Big deal, Kevin."

They tipped his books out of his arms and left him with a scatter of papers to collect.

"We'll see you tomorrow, Kev. Don't forget your lunch money."

By the end of the day, Kevin had forgotten there was a reason to dread going to bed.

"Nothing," he said to himself as he settled between the sheets, "could be worse than today."

The giant snakes came back. This time they crawled up to the front door and slid beneath it. They came under the back door and through the bathroom drains. They slid down the hall to Kevin's door and bumped against the doorknob. Terrorized, Kevin buried his head under the covers. The snakes slid under his bed and came up along the walls. Kevin could feel them hunting through the rumpled blankets. When they found Kevin, they pushed their mirrors against his skin, cold and sharp and insistent. Kevin moaned. He kept his face hidden in the pillow until one very insistent poke forced him to turn over. He looked into one of the mirrors and saw a reflection of his day.

Over and over he watched himself handing over his money to the older boys. He writhed with misery and embarrassment as his ice-cream sandwich flew through the air, and again and again he watched the sneaker stamp down on it. He heard the whole lunchroom laughing in muffled roars like the noise of an underground train.

"Big man of the sixth grade, Kevin?" He was surrounded by high-school students, and he saw himself with their contempt and disgust. He relived every horrible scene of the day, and there was no relief. He saw himself bullying smaller kids and felt no surge of arrogance and power. Instead, he watched from their eyes, and he looked hateful and insecure. He didn't look tough. When he was trying hardest to look tough, he only looked ridiculous.

Mesmerized by the mirror, Kevin watched his whole day pass over and over until he had seen it from the viewpoint of every person he'd encountered and felt every person's opinion.

In the morning, he was exhausted. He dragged himself out of bed and made his way into the kitchen on shaking legs.

"Mom, I don't feel well. I don't want to go to school today."

His mother laughed. "Only one day and already school makes you sick? Go get your clothes on. There's nothing the matter with you that breakfast won't cure."

The days passed. The nights passed, too, but more slowly. No matter what he did, Kevin spent each night reviewing his actions with loathing. Every night the snakes came and prodded him with their mirrors until he dragged his face out of the pillow. In miserable and unavoidable detail, he watched himself through other people's eyes. Inevitably, anyone who noticed him did so with contempt or malicious amusement or loathing. The mildest emotion he ever registered was distaste from his science teacher. No one was ever impressed by him; no one ever admired him. No one thought him good-looking or fashionably dressed.

Most unfair of all, he never once saw himself through the eyes of his friends. He would have protested this, he would have protested everything, but who was there to protest to? Instead, he tried to sound out his friends. He asked them about their dreams but lied about his own. Some of the other kids had had nightmares, but they didn't sound anything like his. Of course, how was he to know? If he was lying, maybe they were, too. He began asking trick questions, hoping to catch them in a lie, but this earned him a few strange looks, and he and his friends drifted further apart. They shared no classes, not even lunch, and somehow it was easy to avoid meeting them after school. Kevin found that if he went straight home and sat in his room, those hours at least would not show up in the mirrors at night.

Why, though, did everyone hate him so much? Why did no one ever think anything good about him? Couldn't he at least dream about what his friends thought, just once?

The apartment was locked the next day when he got home. His mother wouldn't be back for hours, so Kevin left his books by the door and went to look for the gang. They were surprised to see him, but they made room for him at the top of the fence next to the play lot. They spent the afternoon together. They stole a basketball from one of the littler kids and shot baskets for a while. Then they wandered down to the vacant lot by the train tracks and smoked cigarettes that Jerry had taken from his father. The rest of the gang wanted to go to Walgreen's to see if they could lift some candy, but Kevin backed out. He had an idea already that his dreams would be bad. He could guess what the people in Walgreen's would think of him. He went home. He did his homework and ate dinner and went to bed.

That night, watching himself in the mirror, he saw himself through his friends' eyes. None of his friends liked him much. Since the first day of school, when they had watched him fork over his lunch money, they'd been embarrassed to have him around. Kevin wasn't cool. He was a nobody. Every day the high school kids asked him for money, and every day Kevin handed it over just like all the other nobodies in the school.

In the morning, Kevin put his clothes on and, desperately miserable, headed to school. The first bell hadn't rung yet, and the yard was full of people talking about their boyfriends or girlfriends or future or ex boyfriends or girlfriends. Everybody was making plans for the weekend. Kevin couldn't face his friends after the previous night's revelations. He turned left and walked around the school to the front entrance, one that was almost never used. It was deep in a recess formed by the gymnasium wall on one side and three stories of classrooms on the other. The sunlight passed right by without stopping. The wind swirled a couple of pieces of paper and a pop can in a corner against the steps while Kevin sat on the cold concrete steps and thought about how a perfectly normal life can turn into a disaster and all it takes is two weeks in the seventh grade.

The bell rang. Kevin went inside. He dumped his books in his locker and moused his way through another day. He'd never done homework in the sixth grade, but he did it now. There was nothing else to occupy his time as he sat alone in his room every afternoon. And he found that he liked it. He liked the orderliness of mathematics once he understood the rules, and he got almost the same kick out of solving problems that he used to get stealing candy from Walgreen's. He wished his life were as easy to work as a math problem.

By using the school's front entrance, Kevin had avoided the high-school boys who usually relieved him of his lunch money. Having enough money for a regular lunch should have been a bright spot in his day. Unfortunately, he met one of the older boys as he was leaving the lunchroom. The older boy looked down at Kevin's substantial lunch and shook his head back and forth. Kevin scuttled away, realizing that he should have settled for an ice-cream bar; the hamburger stuck in his throat.

That night, when the snakes held up their mirrors, Kevin saw himself slinking down a school hallway, using his notebook as a shield. He was concentrating so hard on anonymity that it was only a particularly conscientious teacher who would have noticed him. Kevin felt the teacher's ripple of curiosity and distaste for the cringing figure. Then the dream moved on.

In the morning, Kevin thought there had been something familiar about that scurrying person in the dream. Of course it had to be familiar; he was watching himself. But there was something beyond that. When he got to school, he slipped around the building, looking for other open entrances. He had cheated the older boys of his lunch money the day before. They would be looking for him that morning. He sat on the steps on the far side of the gymnasium and thought about his problems until the bell rang.

For the next week, Kevin entered the school by various

doors. He went through the music room door. He waited once for the late bell to ring and snuck into the building through the auto shop. The older boys glared at him in the lunchroom, but Kevin was safe while in the building, and the junior high let out half an hour earlier than the high school. One of the gym doors didn't close properly, so Kevin slipped in that way twice. After school, he headed straight home without stopping to hassle any of the smaller kids. Seeing himself through those kids' eyes every night had taken the fun out of the bullying. Kevin's goal was to get through the day with no one noticing him at all.

While sitting alone in his room for hours, Kevin thought about his nightmares. The crouching mousy figure in his dreams rang a distant bell. Kevin racked his brains trying to understand. Finally, the next day, as he waited on the gymnasium steps, the bell rang right inside his head. The sloping walk that he saw in the dreams was the same as the walk of the Jell-O lady, the one he and his friends had been hassling just before school started. The rest of the day passed in a blur. Kevin didn't care what his dreams would be like that night. For the first time he thought he knew where they came from, and he hoped to get rid of them.

After school, he went straight to the bus stop at Fifty-fifth and Hyde Park Boulevard. He checked the passengers getting off every bus. He spent all day Saturday at the bus stop as well. He sat on the bench until the manager at Orly's chased him away. After that, he walked up and down the street, hurrying back to the bench whenever a bus arrived. She wasn't there. By Sunday, he was beginning to despair. What if that had been the only day she had ridden the bus? What if she had bought a car? What if, after ruining his life forever, she'd decided to move to Ohio or someplace like that? He walked up Blackstone Avenue trying to find her apartment building, but couldn't pick it out. Maybe he would never find her and he'd be stuck forever slinking down hallways like some sort of deformed rabbit.

He was late for dinner and should have started home, but he kept telling himself he would wait for just one more bus. Finally, he thought he saw her. Maybe. But she was wearing different clothes, a red coat and an orange dress, and she walked differently, swinging her arms and bobbing her chin, humming to herself as she walked. Kevin had seen her the day before but had not recognized her. He still wasn't sure if this was the woman he wanted or not. He followed her down the street. She turned at a familiar corner and headed for a familiar building.

"Wait," Kevin shouted as she put her key in the door.

She turned and recognized Kevin immediately. She laughed in his face.

"No backsies," she said. The door closed and locked behind her.

"Wait, wait!" Kevin threw himself against the door and rattled the lock. Through the dirty glass in the door he saw the woman disappear up the steps inside without looking back. After a moment, he sat down on the steps and hugged his knees. Eventually, he had to go home for dinner, but the next morning, when the woman came out to go to work, he was waiting on the step.

"What, are you still here?" she asked.

"What did you mean, 'no backsies'?" he asked.

"Just what I said. You can't give it back to me. You have to give it to someone else who asks for it."

"But what is it?"

"What do you think? It's a nightmare." She walked down the street.

Kevin met her when she got off the bus that afternoon. "Why did you give it to me?" he asked.

"Because you asked for it. Hassling an old woman and telling her you want whatever she's got. People who ask for it get what's coming to them."

"Then where did you get it?"

She stopped at the corner. She looked down at him and nodded her head as she admitted, "I asked for it."

"How long?"

"How long did I have it? Six years," she said softly.

Kevin rocked back in horror.

"And you never do get all the way rid of it. Spend time with that nightmare, and you can always see yourself in other people's eyes. Even now, people look at me and think I shouldn't wear a red coat and an orange dress, and I say to myself, 'Hey, I don't care what they think as long as they don't think it in my dreams.'"

"But it's only ever bad things. Why not any good things?" Kevin pleaded.

The woman shrugged. "That's why it's a nightmare."

She looked at Kevin sadly. "Better you than me," she said. Then she walked away, and this time Kevin didn't follow.

His thoughts ran through his head in circles. Six years. I'll be old. Six years, and she only got rid of it because she ran into an idiot like me. How many people that stupid can there be in the world? What if I never get rid of it? What if all the people in the world who are stupid enough to ask have already had it once and I was the very last dummy?

Kevin had heard that there's a sucker born every minute. Maybe the next sucker was just being born, and Kevin would have to wait until he or she grew up enough to say, "Hey, gimme that nightmare. It's just what I always wanted."

Kevin went home. He ate his supper without a word and headed to his room to do his homework. His mother looked with concern at the dark circles under his eyes, but Kevin was too steeped in misery to care. That night he turned a resigned face to the dream mirrors. The woman in the red coat didn't appear, but the disgust of the manager at Orly's oozed over Kevin and stuck like tar.

The next day was Monday. Kevin had run out of open doors at school, so he was forced to begin the cycle again with the main entrance and hope the high-school boys had forgotten him. As he rounded that corner from sunlight to shade, he was momentarily blinded. Shadow figures knocked his books out of his hands and pushed him against the wall.

"Hey, Kev," said a voice out of the dark, "you haven't been in the yard lately. We missed you."

Hunching his shoulders, Kevin could only think of how this scene would reappear in miserable dreams. He didn't really pay attention to what the older boy was saying.

"We were beginning to think you didn't like us, Kev. You do still like us, don't you?"

"Huh? Oh, yeah, sure."

"Doesn't sound real sincere. Tell you what, why don't you give us a token of your esteem?"

"What?"

The older boy held out his hand. "Hand it over, Kevin. Empty those pockets. Whatever you got, I want."

"You want . . . ?" He stopped in confusion and then was tongue-tied with rage. That was his chance. Maybe the only chance he'd ever have and he'd blown it. Now the boy leaned closer. He was going to ask again, but this time he would be specific. He wanted Kevin's lunch money, and Kevin was going to have the nightmare for the rest of his life. Kevin wanted to bang his own head against the wall he was so frustrated, but then, to Kevin's relief, the older boy repeated himself.

"Whatever you got, Kevin, I want. Do you understand?" He clenched his hand into a fist, then opened it again, palm up.

"Yeah," said Kevin, "yeah, sure." He cupped his hand around invisible Jell-O and tossed it into the older boy's waiting hand. "It's all yours," he said, and ran for the school doors as the bell rang.

THE BAKER KING

Once upon a time, there was a very small kingdom that consisted of a single island just off the coast of the mainland. The island and kingdom both were called Monemvassia. *Monem* meant "one" and *vassia* meant "way," and truly there was only one way to reach the Monemvassians. All visitors had to come in at the harbor gate. Only at the harbor was there a break in the cliffs that rose straight out of the sea to form the island. One could get to the island by boat, or one could walk across a bank of sand during low tide, but the harbor gate was the only door to town.

Once you passed through the harbor gate, there were stairs to climb that led up the sides of the island to the very top, where there were various flat spots planted with olive and eucalyptus trees and grapevines and small stone houses. The residents of Monemvassia fished, and they cultivated olives and wine, and many of them spent their days carving wooden spindles out of the local eucalyptus trees. The wooden spools they sent off to the mainland to trade for things that didn't grow on the island. Most people in the kingdom were happy. Some people attributed this to the fact that Monemvassia was the only known kingdom that had no king.

The old king had sent his only child off to school to be educated in kingly ways and then had unfortunately caught a chill while out fishing. Before the king's councillors had a chance to ask, "By the way, to which institution of kingly learning was the crown prince sent?" the old king had died, and the councillors were stuck. There were some angry words exchanged about the foolishness of letting the king choose a school for his son and send him off without informing the council, but the prime minister explained that the old king had thought that the crown prince deserved a little privacy before he became king and gave it all up for the public life.

"Well, he's certainly got his privacy now," said one minister. "He's so private we don't know where he is."

Someone suggested advertising in the international newspapers, but the rest of the council thought that was undignified. Finally they decided to do nothing. Just wait. Surely the prince would send a letter home to say whether he liked school, and when he did that, the council could check the return address. Then they would send someone to fetch home the new king of Monemvassia. It was an exceptional plan, approved by the entire council. They informed the public that while the king was away at school, they would act as regents. There were important decisions to be made and very few restrictions on the council's power. They couldn't increase the taxes, and they couldn't call out the army, but they could collect taxes that were already levied, and they were authorized to disburse money from the royal treasury. They made up a budget for the upcoming year. They organized the annual summer spool festival, and they waited.

Nine years passed, and they were still waiting. The prince hadn't written home. The councillors kept thinking that they would hold off just a few more months before making any decisions that they might regret. Meanwhile, the citizens of Monemvassia were the happiest of any country in the area. In the intervening nine years, there had been revolutions in other countries and several wars. Monemvassia was surrounded by democracies, and dictatorships, and one communist state. But Monemvassia itself was peaceful and prosperous. Unable to call up the army, the council had been circumspect in its foreign policy, and of course, taxes hadn't been raised since the old king died. The wooden spool trade was booming. The council felt secure and decided to wait another year before addressing the problem of the missing prince. Surely by then he would have finished his education and be on his way home to take the throne.

When a letter arrived addressed to the king's council, the ministers were overjoyed, thinking that at last the prince had sent word. Unfortunately the letter was not from the prince. It was from a man named Spiro Popodoupaoulas.

In the letter, he explained that it had come to his attention that the king of Monemvassia had been missing for nine years. Having only just realized that the kingdom was without any sort of sovereign guidance, a most deplorable and in this case remediable state, he was offering himself as a replacement for their delinquent monarch. He and his associates would arrive on the tenth of the following month to assume all rights and responsibilities of government. He wished to have the coronation ceremony the day he arrived, and there should be plenty of malmsey on hand to serve guests. The council should have ready suitable residences for himself and his many, many associates. He would send more details with future messengers. He signed his letter "Most Sincerely, Spiro Popodoupaoulas the First."

"Spiro Popodoupaoulas," said one minister. "Is that the bandit Spiro the Unpopular who has been holding up trade in the inland mountains?"

"The same," said another minister.

"I don't understand what he wants."

"He wants to be king," the minister of finance explained.

"But we have a king." The minister of the royal wardrobe was over ninety, and sometimes things had to be explained to him very carefully.

"What's this about associates?" asked the minister of the armed forces, who hadn't had a lot to do in the last decade and spent most of his time fishing.

"I think that means army," said the minister of finance, with whom the minister of the armed forces usually fished.

"This is very bad." It was going to interrupt the fishing.

"What are we going to do?"

"Call up the army?" the minister of finance suggested.

"Can't do it without a royal decree," said the minister of the armed forces. "Wouldn't do much good if we did. They haven't trained in ten years."

"Oh, dear."

"Does anyone have any suggestions?" asked the prime minister.

The sun was shining, and the air was brisk. Orvis, who was the king's minister of cultural events (that meant he organized Monemvassia's annual festival to celebrate spool making), walked down the hill from the palace with the cloth of his ministerial robes going *fphliit, fphliit, fphliit* against his legs. He watched his feet stamp in the cobblestones and rehearsed in his head the cutting speech he should have addressed to the council. It had taken him hours of careful work to convince them of the threat of this Spiro Popodoupaoulas and his private army. More careful work had convinced the council that only a new king, one that could call up an army, would do in this crisis, and if the true king arrived later, the substitute could always abdicate. That was a concession to the conservatives. Of course, the new king should have an impeccable character and a great deal of experience. He should be selected from the council, for example. He should be a minister who was used to responsibility.

After hours of meandering debate, Orvis had gently, gently suggested a nomination of two candidates for kingship to be voted on the following Friday. His suggestion was taken, but neither of the candidates, neither of them, was Orvis!

Fphliit, fphliit went the council robes, and *smack smack* his feet jarred on the cobblestones until he ran *bang* into someone hard. There was a tricky moment when a collection of white objects flew through the air, before the world settled down and the white things turned out to be cake boxes. Orvis sat up from where he had fallen and looked at the heavyset master baker who had been his partner in the collision.

"You should have watched where you're going," snapped Orvis.

"One of us should have been watching," said the baker. "Good thing those cake boxes are empty."

"A very good thing," said Orvis stiffly. "We might have had quite a mess." He was thinking of his council robe. It was dark purple, and he was particular about its neatness.

"We're in luck, I guess," said the baker, and Orvis agreed, each thinking it was the other who had been lucky.

Some of the flour on the baker's apron had brushed off on the purple ministerial robe, and Orvis asked the man if he had a handkerchief to get it off. The baker handed Orvis a handkerchief even more covered with flour than he was himself. Orvis handed it back and stepped into the bakery to find something more suitable.

The bakery was a large room with a counter near the door to separate the bakers from the customers. Behind the counter were the huge ovens and the racks for the fresh breads and pastries. Beyond them were doors leading to the cold storage rooms cut into the solid rock that was under the bakery and all the buildings in Monemvassia. While Orvis was swatting at his robe with a clean handkerchief, a young man stepped out of one of these doors carrying a limp snake. The bakers left a wide path between the young man and the door. The only person who didn't move out of the way was Orvis, who was busy.

"Excuse me, sir,"

"Yes?" Orvis looked up. He froze when he saw the snake, but Orvis didn't jump back in fright the way someone less attached to his dignity might have done.

"Young man, that is a poisonous snake you have in your hand."

"Yes, sir, it's asleep."

"Oh?"

"Yes, sir," the journeyman baker explained. "They crawl into the cold storage pantries sometimes and fall asleep there. I like to pick them up and carry them away before they wake up enough to eat anything."

"Why not kill them?" It seemed like a more obvious solution to Orvis.

"Well, they eat the seagull eggs, sir, and that keeps the seagull population down."

Orvis had to agree that anything that got rid of seagulls couldn't be all bad. Seagulls were a terrible pest in Monemvassia. They came in with the fishing ships and roosted all over the island, leaving dirty streaks on the laundry hung up to dry and on the one statue in the kingdom, the first king of Monemvassia, holding a eucalyptus spool in one hand.

"So go ahead and get rid of it then," said Orvis, and the young man disappeared through the bakery door.

Orvis returned the handkerchief to its owner and was about to leave when one of the master bakers coughed politely.

"Excuse me, Minister, but I wonder if you could tell us

any news. There have been rumors about a bandit, Spiro the Unpopular."

"Oh?" said Orvis at his most haughty.

"Well, yes," said the baker. "And you being a minister and no doubt a very important man, I was sure that if there were anything to be concerned about, you would surely know." This just shows that the master baker was a smart man. It was no wonder his bakery was the largest on the island.

"My good man," said Orvis, "let me lay your fears to rest." And he proceeded to tell the baker all the reasons why he had nothing to worry about, which only made the old baker more nervous than ever. Orvis was still going on when the journeyman baker returned from having disposed of the cliff snake.

"Any news from the king?" he asked.

Orvis went back to being silent and haughty. "No," he said, and turned to go.

"Wonder if anyone will recognize him when he shows up," said the journeyman. "You'd think anyone at all could arrive and say that he was the king."

Orvis paused in the doorway.

"I could be king myself," said the young man, and he puffed out his chest and struck a royal pose that was spoiled by the smile on his face. The rest of the bakery laughed.

"All hail King Nele," called out someone in the back.

Orvis looked at the young baker thoughtfully. Most Monemvassians had broad shoulders and short legs. Their hair tended to be thick and dark and curly. But the old king and his son had had high foreheads and straightish fair hair. In the king's case, the hair had wisped away, leaving his pink skin to show through. The young baker, with his sandy-colored hair and his fair skin, could in fact pass for the missing king.

Someone bumped into Orvis, who was still blocking the bakery door. Distracted by his thoughts, the minister of cultural events was more polite than usual. He excused himself and hurried away. By the time he got home, he was quite pleased with the plan he had in mind—so pleased that when his daughter asked if he would take her to the puppet show the following month at the summer spool festival, he actually agreed, to his daughter's surprise. She had expected the same answer he gave every year, which was absolutely not—he spent too much time organizing the event to waste money attending it himself. (The ministry of cultural events did not pay well. No position on the council did.)

That evening, Nele and the other employees filed out of the bakery at closing time. All of them carried the leftover bread that they would have for dinner. As Nele walked down the street toward his home, someone fell into step beside him. He assumed it was his friend Bet, but when he looked, he saw it was Orvis, minister of cultural events. Orvis asked if Nele had just a few minutes to talk.

Orvis wanted to know if Nele had any family. Nele said he had none. What had Nele's father done before he died? Nele explained that he had been apprenticed before he had any clear idea of how his father occupied his time. Orvis smiled. And did Nele remember where he had lived before he had been apprenticed? Nele did not. It was a big house with a wonderful garden, but more he couldn't say. Orvis rubbed his hands in delight and explained that he had considered what Nele had said in jest earlier that day, and perhaps it was true. Perhaps Nele was the missing king and didn't know it.

Nele looked at him in blank consternation. His eyes were round, and Orvis began to think maybe the boy was not very bright. That suited Orvis.

Someone standing beside them gave a low whistle. It was Bet. "King Nele," said Bet. "What a laugh."

Orvis jumped. He hadn't realized that he and Nele were not alone. "I remind you, young man, that the missing king's given name was Maninele."

"So?" said Bet.

"Well, it could very easily have been shortened to Nele. We won't say any more about it now," he said. "Let me give you a silver piece ..." He looked at Nele, who was still standing like a lump. He handed the silver piece to Bet instead. "To keep your thoughts to yourself," Orvis said. He looked at Bet significantly and left.

"What do you think of that?" Bet asked Nele.

"What I think," said Nele, "is that if that man is my councillor, I wouldn't want to be king."

"Definitely on the sneaky side," said Bet. "What are you going to do?"

"I'm going to have wine and cheese with my dinner tonight and share it with you." He swept the silver coin out of Bet's hand and tossed it in the air. "He can't take back what we've already eaten."

The next morning, Bet was careful to remind the other bakers of Nele's joke the day before. With elaborate courtesy, he addressed him as King Nele. The bakers and their early-morning customers laughed, and for the rest of the day people bowed and called King Nele to please come collect the snakes from the pantry and bring up baking supplies when he was done. King Nele waved his hands, declaring that it would be his royal pleasure to haul sacks of flour.

But that evening, when all the bread was sold and the shop was closed, Nele went to see Orvis in his home on the east side of the island. Nele didn't like the house very much. Most of the houses on Monemvassia were small and dark, built with thick stone walls and small windows. But unlike its neighbors, this house had no garden, no patio, no pleasant place to sit on warm evenings. Instead, Nele and Orvis sat in a small room behind the kitchen. Previously it had been a garden, but it had been roofed over and turned into Orvis's private office. Nele thought the minister's sharp and unpleasant personality might have been fostered by too much paperwork about parades, read in a room that smelled like last week's fish and onion dinner.

Orvis asked Nele a lot of questions about his childhood that Nele answered in short, not very clever sentences. It pleased Orvis that Nele seemed not too bright and would make an easily malleable king. After all, Orvis thought, who knew more about puppet shows than a man who had planned them every summer for years?

"Now, you don't remember much of your father, right?"

"Right."

"So you don't know for sure that he wasn't the king of Monemvassia, right?"

"Right."

"So he could have been king?"

"I suppose."

"Let's say he is."

"Okay."

"So this is what your childhood was like," and Orvis

explained everything in detail. Every few sentences, he asked Nele to repeat back what he had heard. Nele made a lot of mistakes, but eventually seemed to get the material down pat. Orvis gave him another silver coin and told him to come back the next evening.

In the morning, he convinced the council to delay the vote on the two nominees for kingship. He suggested they wait a few more weeks just in case the true king actually arrived. After all, the militia could be called out right up to the last minute and nobody needed to know that they would be armed only with boat hooks and cooking knives. After nine years, waiting was a habit the council found hard to break. The ministers agreed to hold off the vote until Spiro's arrival was imminent.

Every night, Orvis drilled Nele. Every day, he racked his brains to come up with a way to explain how the king of Monemvassia could show up as an employee in a local bakery. He would have liked to pretend that Nele, the baker, had fallen off a cliff, and that his candidate for king was someone entirely new, but he didn't think Nele was smart enough to keep up with the pretense. And Monemvassia was a small enough island that there were too many people who were bound to recognize him.

"Well," Nele suggested one night, "maybe the real king fell out of the carriage and got lost and the baker took him in?"

"I told you to stop saying 'the real king,' " Orvis snapped. "You are the real king. Remember that."

"Right," said Nele sheepishly. "Well, maybe the real, I mean maybe I didn't fall out of the carriage. Maybe I jumped out because I didn't want to be king."

"That's ridiculous," snarled Orvis. "And it would be hard to explain how your father's name came to be signed on your apprentice papers." Every possible plan fell to pieces when it struck the apprentice papers. Each apprenticeship in the kingdom was recorded in the Monemvassia archives, with the name of the apprentice as well as his parent or guardian's signature.

"Nah," said Nele. "My dad's name isn't on mine. One of the neighbors brought me in and signed the papers because my dad was sick."

"Oh?" said Orvis.

"Yeah," said Nele, at his most innocent. "Maybe you could tell everyone that the old king didn't really send the prince off to school. He got one of his ministers to take me, I mean him, I mean me, down to the bakery and sign me up as an apprentice. Maybe he wanted the prince, you know, to get an idea of everyday life."

Orvis thought for a moment. "Much too far-fetched," he said. "That sort of thing could never have happened." He outlined instead a story in which the crown prince fell out of the carriage and was found lost by a good citizen who took him to the bakery to learn a trade. The next night, he started drilling Nele on authenticating details.

Meanwhile, the bandit king, Spiro the Unpopular, had been getting closer and closer. He had been sending messages about his whereabouts and further details of his billeting requirements. He sent a long list of loyal retainers that he suggested be put up in the royal palace. The king's councillors blanched, mainly because there wasn't a royal palace. The king had always lived in a house only slightly larger than that of a common citizen in Monemvassia. It was distinguished by the pleasantness of its gardens, not by the luxury of its rooms.

"No matter," said the messenger who had carried Spiro's letter. "I'm sure he would have wanted to build a whole new palace anyway."

The council went on debating the relative merits of the two chosen royal candidates, and Spiro the Unpopular got closer. Finally, Spiro's army arrived on the edge of the sandbar leading to the harbor gate. The tide was rising fast so he sent a message by boat to say that he would cross to the island at low tide the following morning and he hoped the royal palace was ready.

Low tide the next day wasn't until ten o'clock. The council agreed to meet before then to settle the question of kings once and for all. Orvis spent the night drilling Nele until he was sure that if the half-wit would just keep to the script, then Orvis would be the next prime minister and the power behind the throne.

At eight-fifteen the following morning, he checked to make sure that all the councillors were in their seats and waiting for the prime minister to call the meeting to order. He threw open the council room doors and marched in with his purple ministerial robe billowing behind him and announced, after waving one arm in a theatrical manner that produced a satisfying shushing noise from the robe, that he had found the king.

He swept up and down the council chamber as he explained the peculiar but providential intuition that made him think that the absent king might in fact be under their very noses.

"And so," he said, waving his arms as he spoke, because waving made him feel grand and impressive, "I have carefully scrutinized each citizen of our kingdom, examined each and every one, from the oldest to the very youngest, looking"—he put on his most sincere expression—"for our dear lost prince." He shook his arms one more time. "And I have found"—he paused—"our king."

The minister of finance sat with his arms crossed and looked unimpressed. The prime minister looked very grave.

"So," said Orvis briskly, "we can skip the vote electing a new king and move right to calling out the militia."

"Doesn't the king want to do that himself?" asked one minister.

"Couldn't we, uh, meet the king?" asked the minister for trade.

"Like to, uh, discuss a few things with him," said the minister of the armed forces.

"Like what he's going to wear to the coronation," mumbled the minister of the royal wardrobe to himself.

"Like where he's been for nine years," said the prime minister.

"Right," said Orvis. "I'll be back in a moment." And he stalked back out of the council room doors toward the anteroom where he had left Nele. He was followed by every single councillor, because none of them wanted to wait to meet this unknown king.

When the whole crowd of ministers had squeezed into the anteroom, they found that besides themselves, it was empty. No one else was there. The councillors looked askance at Orvis, who swore that the king had been left there moments before he, Orvis, had gone to address the council.

"God help us, we've lost him again," said one minister.

"Quick," shouted Orvis, flapping his arms in their purple

sleeves, "everyone spread out and look for him! He has to be here somewhere!"

Monemvassia's council building was only slightly larger than the royal residence (it was likewise distinguished by its fine garden), so there were not many rooms to search. Nele was quickly found in the throne room bent over the throne and examining it closely. He turned to face Orvis when he and the other ministers crowded through the door.

"You know," said Nele, "there's a terrible curse on this chair. I don't think I want to sit on it after all." And he pushed past the ministers and out the door. "Sorry," he said to Orvis as he passed.

Well, all the ministers knew about the curse, of course. It promised death and destruction to any usurper who sat on Monemvassia's throne. No one was sure if it was just a story or not, but even if it was a real curse, surely it wouldn't bother the true heir to the throne . . . if he was the true heir to the throne. The ministers turned as one to look at Orvis.

Orvis turned pink. "Perhaps," he said in a very small voice, "I was incorrect." But he got no further with an explanation before Spiro the Unpopular arrived, pushing his way through the crowd of purple robes much the same way he had pushed through the tide before it had left the sandbar completely. He was wet to the knees and not in a happy mood.

"At least," he said, "you are waiting for me in the throne room."

No one explained why, because no one had time. Spiro stamped to the front of the room and up the steps to the throne.

He said, "I, Spiro the Popular, declare myself king of Monemvassia, henceforth to be known as Spiroland," and he plumped his ample bottom down on the seat cushion.

Almost immediately he fell over dead, bitten by the cliff snake that Nele had left sleeping right there on that cushion. The snake had not been happy to have his sleep interrupted by anything as ample and invasive as Spiro's bottom, and after sinking both fangs into a particularly fleshy part of it, the snake slipped off the edge of the cushions and under the seat of the throne to continue its nap, hidden by the drapery. No one but the prime minister saw it go.

The king's ministers one and all stared at Spiro. Clearly the curse was a real one and very powerful, too. Very quietly they returned to the council chamber to review their options. Both candidates for the kingship withdrew their nominations.

"So we can't call out the royal militia?" said the minister of finance.

"Not legally," said the minister of armed forces.

"Oh, dear," said the minister of the royal wardrobe, and for once all the other ministers agreed with him.

"What do you think the bandits will do when they hear Spiro is dead?"

"Loot the town, probably," said the minister of the armed forces with a sigh.

"We could close the harbor gate and keep them out," suggested the minister of finance.

"Did that, actually," said the minister of the armed forces.

"So we'll starve instead," said the minister of trade.

"Surely we have fish and olives and grapes to eat?" said the minister of finance.

"Not a balanced diet," said the minister of health. "The children will all have runny noses."

"Oh, dear," said the minister of the royal wardrobe.

A breathless messenger burst through the council chamber's doors. "The bandits, the bandits," he gasped.

"Yes, yes," said the minister of the royal wardrobe, "we already know all about the bandits."

"They're leaving," said the messenger. It seemed that the bandits were a superstitious bunch, and when they heard about the scene in the throne room, they had remembered that they hadn't been keen to take over a kingdom of fish and wooden spools anyway. They were heading back to the mountains to hold up trade. As for Spiro, he had been called the Unpopular for a reason. No one much cared what happened to him.

After a few moments of relieved discussion, the prime minister asked, "Where's that boy, Orvis? The one you said was king?"

Orvis with a lot of smooth talking managed to convince the council that it had all been a terrible mistake, an error on his part, an unfortunate misunderstanding. The council decided that they had disposed of Spiro so easily that they really didn't need a king after all. The prime minister recommended that they keep the position open, nonetheless, just in case the true king someday returned.

That afternoon, Nele had a visitor at the bakery, come to remind him that only members of the council and the royal family knew about the curse.

"Oops," said Nele.

"I don't think anyone else has thought about it," said

the prime minister. "I take it that you have enjoyed your apprenticeship?"

"I have," said Nele.

"You'll let me know if you change your mind about being king?"

"I will," said Nele. "Call me if you need me again?"

"Yes," said his prime minister.

Orvis also came to see Nele. He stopped him after work while he walked down the dark street toward home. Orvis wanted to explain that he wasn't really the king and wasn't on any account to mention the king business to anyone. He said everything very slowly, and he said it twice to make sure Nele understood. Once again, he'd failed to notice Bet standing in the shadows until Bet stepped forward and suggested that a gold piece might keep everyone's mouth shut.

Orvis handed over the gold piece and went home in a terrible mood. When his daughter asked about the puppet show, he snapped that of course they wouldn't go. Spend good money on a puppet show? He was sick to death of them and hoped never to see another.

When Orvis was gone, Bet said, "He does think you're an idiot, doesn't he?"

"He's got a good reason," said Nele, and described the scene in the throne room. The two young bakers walked down the street with their arms filled with leftover bread, laughing.

"What shall we do with our gold coin?" asked Bet.

"Same as we did with the silver ones, I think," said Nele. They had wine and cheese for dinner every night for a month, and with the money left over they went to the puppet show. The bakers at the Monemvassia bakery still kidded Nele about his brief career as the crown prince and, much to Orvis's disgust, someone wrote the whole business down and called it the story of the baker king.

Megan Whalen Turner is the author of the 1997 Newbery Honor Book *The Thief*, also available from Puffin. She is a graduate of the University of Chicago, where she majored in English language and literature. She and her husband, a professor, live with their children in Maryland.